GOOD GIRL

THE SIREN ISLAND SERIES, BOOK ONE

TRICIA O'MALLEY

LOVEWRITE PUBLISHING

Good Girl
The Siren Island Series
Book One

Cover Design:
Alchemy Book Covers
Editor:
Elayne Morgan

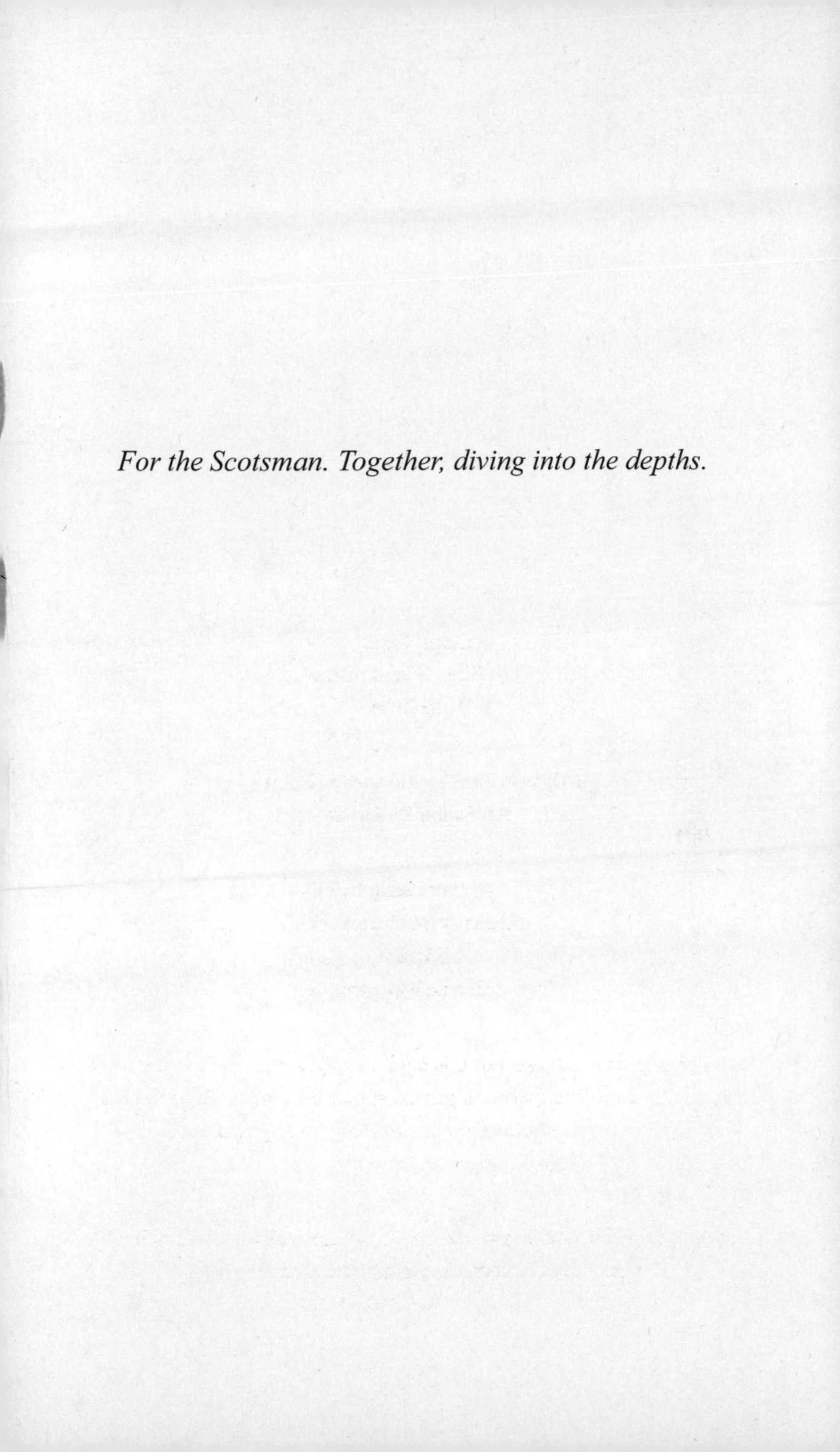

For the Scotsman. Together, diving into the depths.

“They ask us to sing our songs again.”
– Oracle of Mermaids

CHAPTER 1

"Business or pleasure?"

"Business," Sam said automatically, her fingers tightening on the strap of the laptop case that rarely left her shoulder.

"And what is your business on Siren Island?" The customs agent spoke with a bouncy cadence, his words slow and richly rounded, the music of the islands flowing through his voice.

"I… I mean, pleasure," Sam said, startled to realize it was true. A drop of sweat slipped between her shoulder blades. That morning, in a haze of *what-the-hell-am-I-doing,* she'd donned what she'd come to term her Air Barbie uniform. It had breezed her through most airports in the world, straight into whatever hotel finance meetings she was attending, and had earned her more than her fair share of upgrades .

Impeccably tailored slacks? Check. Tasteful

diamond stud earrings? Check. And a silk blouse in a muted color – not too bright, as she'd learned that the men in the board meetings she ran often took a power color as an invitation to flirt.

Though why she'd added her diaphanous silk scarf and patent leather sling-backs to the outfit, Sam had no clue.

Her plane wouldn't be landing in a fiercely air-conditioned airport with valets to whisk her luggage away as she went from one perfectly manicured space to the next. Oh no. Not even close.

Instead, here she was holding up a line of sweaty, boisterous passengers who all seemed to have overindulged on the plane ride down to whichever hotel's all-inclusive vacation package they'd signed up for. The sun, an angry unrepentant dictator, broiled them all with her cruel rays.

"Which is it, ma'am? Business or pleasure?" The customs agent regarded her carefully, and it annoyed Sam to see not even a sheen of sweat on the man's face, though he wore neatly pressed khaki pants and a button-down shirt. Why were there no enclosed rooms in this hut of an airport? Samantha knew for a fact that the island had access to the internet; surely they'd learned of the invention of air conditioning by now.

"Pleasure. My apologies. I travel so much for work that I forgot this trip was for pleasure," Sam said, sweeping her tastefully highlighted auburn hair over her shoulder and flashing the agent the smile that had opened more than one door for her in the past.

"That's a shame, ma'am. One should never forget to take time for pleasure." The agent's voice never changed, but something flashed in his eyes for just a moment – a warm male appreciation that, for once, didn't feel predatory. Sam got the impression that he enjoyed all women. When she heard him begin flirting with the lady behind her, who sported a fanny pack and an unruly swath of grey hair, her assumption was confirmed.

His words followed her as she tapped her foot impatiently by the single-loop baggage conveyor belt, and Sam's annoyance reached peak levels as another passenger jostled her to peer over her shoulder.

"I really hope they didn't lose our bags this time. I swear, Carl, every time we come here something gets lost."

Then why did they still come here? Sam wondered in frustration, deliberately spreading her elbows a bit to strike a power pose – the one she used in crowds to force people to step away from her a bit.

For that matter, what was *she* even doing here? As Sam's thoughts flashed back over the last forty-eight hours, sweat began to drip in earnest down her back, and she was certain she could actually feel the blood pumping through her heart. Gulping for air, she looked around wildly. What this airport needed was some fans.

The sunlight seemed to get brighter and the eager laughter of the crowd around her sounded like the braying of mules. The faces and laughter and heat and sweat all pressed on her until Sam turned to run – only to find herself trapped by the crowd. Panic skittered its way up her throat and she gasped, trying to draw a breath against the warm press of bodies pushing toward the bags that now belched from a small flap-covered hole in the wall.

A hand closed on hers and Sam's gaze slammed into cool blue eyes – the color of the sea – and a calm wave of energy seemed to pour through her. She lost herself in the reassuring smile of a woman, a peaceful oasis of calm, who pulled her through the crowd.

"Sit." Samantha's butt had barely touched the seat when the woman unceremoniously pushed Sam's head between her legs. She gulped air, desperately trying to hold her panic attack at bay. The last thing she heard before it all went dark was the woman's voice.

"This one's mine."

CHAPTER 2

"Are you feeling better, Ms. Jameson?" The woman – an angel if she'd ever met one, Samantha had decided – clambered into the dusty driver's seat of a raggedy pick-up truck. She beamed at Sam, who sat wilting in the front seat, holding a frozen bottle of water to the back of her neck.

"I think so," Sam said, willing to sell this woman her first-born if she would just turn the air conditioner on.

"Welcome to Siren Island. I'm Irma Margarite, and I'll be your fearless leader," Irma said with a chuckle.

Despite her embarrassment at being a wilted mess, Sam smiled back at her. "It would be nice to let someone else take the reins for once," Sam admitted.

Digging in her butter-soft leather satchel until she found her quilted Coach sunglasses case, Sam slipped the dark shades over her eyes. Feeling calmer behind the glasses, she studied the woman next to her, who chattered briefly to a man in the parking lot, in a language that sounded similar to Spanish.

But still, no air conditioning.

Irma threw back her head and laughed at something he said, her thick braid of salt-and-pepper hair bouncing with her movements, the turquoise bangles at her wrist clinking softly as she shifted the truck into gear. She wore a breezy island dress in the carefree way of women who cared little for what society thought about their bodies. The loose linen dress in the colors of sunset made her look incredibly alluring, and Samantha immediately decided she wanted to be her when she grew up.

Except she was already grown up. Long past it, and on her way toward spinsterhood, as her family enjoyed reminding her. Sam wondered if anyone even used that word anymore – other than her family, of course. Cool air finally sputtered from the dusty vents in the truck's dashboard.

"Why's that?" Irma asked, and Samantha realized she'd repeated her question. Irma shot the truck out into traffic with barely a glance for oncoming vehicles. Sam desperately wanted to ask if the truck's indicators worked, but tamped down the urge. Others often made fun of her for following the rules, but deviating from what was expected of her had only led to massive screw-ups in the past. For years now, she'd kept her nose to the grindstone and worked tirelessly to prove to everyone that a Jameson, and a Jameson woman at that, could indeed lead a wildly successful – hell, even enviable – career as the senior accountant and luxury portfolio manager for Paradiso Hotels. It was a career that thumbed its nose in the face of the chosen profession of the Jamesons – the law.

"Why's what?" Sam realized she'd been plucking at her trousers – a sure sign she was stressed – and she involuntarily closed her eyes as they approached a traffic circle at a higher rate of speed than she deemed necessary.

"Why do you want someone else to lead you?" Irma asked, her tone light as she beeped the horn at someone.

"I'm tired." Sam was surprised to hear herself say the words. "I'm just so tired of playing by the rules." She bit her lip and closed her mouth before the entire story came tumbling out of her mouth to this random woman driving her to some god-knows-what bed and breakfast here on a speck of a Caribbean island.

"You're in luck then," Irma said. "We have very few rules at the Laughing Mermaid Guesthouse. You'll have all the time you need to rest up."

Sam feared she'd need more time than the three-week stay she'd impulsively booked yesterday. Her unexpected absence was leaving her company in the lurch, she knew, but after what they'd done Sam was feeling very little loyalty to them anyway. It was unlikely three weeks would be enough to change her life, but maybe – just maybe – she'd get some peace and quiet for once.

"Why did you have an opening for that long? At the last minute? In high season?" Sam blurted, then internally chastised herself. Just because she was the senior accountant overseeing the international accounts of Paradiso Hotels & Villas didn't mean it was any of her business to pry into this woman's business or operating numbers. But in her opinion, for any place to have that much time available for booking at the last minute must mean poor service or something else hellish awaited discovery on the other end.

"We had a cancellation due to a guest's personal emergency. I was a bit flustered, as it is high season, but before I had time to get frustrated your reservation pinged through. It was meant to be," Irma said with a shrug, a smile hovering on her serene face.

Sam suspected this woman didn't do "flustered," but kept her opinion to herself. She was good at that – in fact, it seemed she'd been doing it for much too long. Otherwise Paradiso would have known a thing or two about what Sam would tolerate in her workplace.

Namely, that would *not* be the resident asshole, Christopher, and his shocking promotion to Chief Financial Officer – a position that had long been promised to her, so long as she kept her head down and worked extra hours. Paradiso Hotels had no idea they were about to lose their best accountant – the one who was intimately familiar with all the books for their million-plus dollar rentals. Sam hadn't even quite admitted it to herself yet, so instead of losing her shit when Christopher was named CFO in the huge board meeting yesterday, she'd calmly left, booked the vacation her friend Lola had been pushing on her for ages, and turned off her cell phone.

In that order.

At the time, it had felt amazing. Perhaps it was a bit sad that turning off her cell phone was the most rebellious act Sam had done in years, but there hadn't been much time for her to examine that little nugget of information before the panic had begun clawing its way in. What had she done? Leaving the company for a vacation in the middle of acquiring several new luxury properties was… unheard of. Not just frowned upon, but actually unheard of.

Samantha's networking circle of friends had reminded her repeatedly over the years that she had scored a dream job, one that flew her to fabulous locations all over the world. In other words, they didn't have much sympathy if she wanted to vent when things got stressful. They all said the same thing: Any girl would kill for her job. Except Lola, that is. Lola never said that.

Instead of weathering the storm at her to-die-for job, Sam now found herself sticking to the seat of a woefully under-cooled truck while her company scrambled to handle her absence.

The truck lurched its way to a stop in front of a simple white villa tucked between a row of palms on a hidden dirt road. There'd been no sign for the turnoff to the Laughing Mermaid Guesthouse, and Sam was certain that no guest would ever find their own way down the weaving potholed road to the inn. She'd certainly never find her way back – if she even decided to rent a car. Between packing and steadfastly ignoring the pinging of arriving emails from her open laptop, she'd forgotten about that little detail. Silently cursing Lola and her bohemian friend's love of "off the beaten path" locations, Sam sighed as she peeled herself from the front seat, and stood flapping her blouse against her chest and eyeing the villa wearily.

"Welcome home, Sam. I think you'll find exactly what you're looking for here," Irma said, hefting Sam's bag easily over her shoulder and swinging past her down a mosaic pathway in a cloud of sunset silk and tinkling jewelry.

"I don't know what I'm looking for," Sam called after her.

"Even better."

CHAPTER 3

It wasn't often that Samantha felt intimidated. But there was something about the careless confidence with which Irma held herself – breezing through a shaded passageway, up a flight of cool white stairs, chattering all the while about the island – that left Sam feeling like she'd landed in an alternate universe. One where she wasn't in control, and this exotic grand dame of a woman ran the mothership.

Even though Sam had told Irma she would like someone else to lead for a while, it was a hopeless lie. Sam was as likely to give up her carefully controlled regimen as she was to start spouting poetry and dancing naked in the moonlight.

Some things were as reliable as the rising of the sun each day, and the fact that Samantha Jameson would always follow the rules, work hard, and carefully mold her life into a perfect example of success that even her family couldn't pick apart was one of them.

Or had been, until now.

"Welcome to the Laughing Mermaid, Samantha," Irma said, her eyes creasing at the corners as she smiled at Sam. "This room is called the Dreaming Moon. We hope you'll be happy here."

"The Dreaming Moon?" Samantha almost snorted at the silliness of the name. In her business she knew clients preferred to book rooms with ocean views and easy-to-understand names like Blue Bay or The Palms. The Dreaming Moon was a touch too whimsical, in her opinion.

Irma studied her with those clear blue eyes, and Samantha tugged at her scarf, involuntarily pulling it over her more, as if the silk could hide her from the careful scrutiny she saw in Irma's gaze.

"Yes. You're never too old to dream under the light of a full moon," Irma said, swinging open a thick wooden door to reveal a room that begged for relaxation. Samantha actually felt tension easing from her shoulders as she stepped into the airy room.

Whitewashed stucco walls were set off by brilliantly-colored hooked rugs thrown over cool tile floors. A huge bed, with airy white netting hung from four posters, was tucked under a rounded alcove in the corner. Artwork dappled the walls, from easy black-and-white sketches of mermaids and celestial bodies to boldly-colored oil paintings in streaks of cobalt blue that showcased the ocean in all her moods. Sunlight danced across the floor, streaming in through the gauzy curtains framing the two French doors which Irma moved across the room to throw open.

Samantha sighed audibly as she followed Irma, as if pulled by the call of the waves outside, to stand on the balcony overlooking the prettiest stretch of ocean she'd ever seen. It was funny, Samantha thought as her eyes drank in the sight of the empty beach, surrounded by a lush garden of palms, orchids, and aloe plants: She'd seen her fair share of majestic beaches in her line of work, but there was something about this beach – no, this space – that spoke directly to her soul.

"It's stunning," Samantha breathed.

"Some would even say magickal." Irma winked at Samantha, her arms crossed over her sunset caftan.

"It does feel that way," Samantha said. "Perhaps because it's so uncluttered? I've been to some of the top beaches in the world, but they're always so busy with tourists. This… this is like its own secret slice of heaven." Sam clamped her mouth shut. She must be more worn out than she'd thought, to be this giddy about a beach.

"It's a perfect spot to let go – to be free from life's expectations for a bit," Irma said. "I hope you'll let yourself be free here."

"I'm not sure what you mean by 'be free,'" Samantha said, finding the woman's phrasing a bit odd, but still too distracted by the view to be annoyed.

"Isn't that what a holiday is all about?" Irma asked, those cool blue eyes assessing Sam once more. "To let yourself be free from the roles you play back home?"

"Some would say it isn't role-playing so much as just living your life," Sam countered.

"Ah, well. In that case, I hope you can live your life differently for a little while down here," Irma said, and patted Sam's shoulder gently as she stepped from the balcony. "All the information you need is in the guide-book on the table. I'll leave you to unpack. Please know that both of my daughters and I are always available to answer any of your questions. Rest well, Samantha."

Samantha nodded her thanks and turned back to the ocean, tamping down her annoyance at Irma's words. Who was this woman to imply that Samantha was just role-playing in her life? If a concierge had ever said something like that to a guest at one of their hotels, they would have been written up. Guests didn't want to be reminded of any of their stresses or shortcomings, Sam fumed as she unzipped her suitcase, looking for something more suitable to wear in the humid weather. It was extremely presumptuous of this woman to assume Sam needed to be free from her life. A life that anyone would love to have, she reminded herself.

As she pulled on a tasteful black one-piece suit and grabbed her beach essentials – an iPad, two books, sunscreen, a big floppy hat, and a notepad – Samantha found herself wondering why Irma's words had felt like a criticism. Perhaps she *was* just a little on edge. Or maybe Samantha was looking for criticism? Her whole life she'd been criticized in one form or another – by her family, her ex-fiancé, and now even her work. The one place where she thought she had excelled.

Samantha was reminded of a quote she'd read years ago that had stuck with her. Grabbing her tote, she wandered from her room to follow the stairs down to a softly shaded passageway where a ceramic mermaid pointed the way to the beach. For some reason, now more than ever, the quote zipped around her brain, niggling at her.

Sometimes the only way to win the game is not to play.

Was that what she was doing here? Stepping out of the game? If she removed herself from the constant criticism of her family and the pressures of her job, what would happen? Would Samantha Jameson as she knew her cease to exist?

Or perhaps it was time for the real Samantha Jameson to be born.

CHAPTER 4

Sam wasn't used to deep self-analysis; frankly she rarely had time for anything other than work and a hurried catch-up dinner with Lola when she was in town. Brushing off her deep thoughts with a laugh – Irma clearly had gotten into her head – Samantha strolled into the garden and followed the little winding pathway that led through a small orchid garden to a beach shaded by tall palms.

Delighted to find the beach relatively empty, Samantha carefully chose a lounge chair with a bright turquoise cushion under a palm tree whose leaves fluttered softly in the breeze. Settling in, she pulled her books and notepad from her bag and set them with her water bottle on the table next to the chair. Dutifully applying her reef-safe sunscreen – an environmental side project she'd spearheaded at all their account hotels – Sam relaxed slowly back into the chair. Her eyes drank in the sight of the sun playing across the waves lapping lazily at the shoreline, and she began to relax incrementally. Even if she had hell to go back to when this vacation was over, in this moment Sam felt she'd made the best choice for her – regardless of what anyone else thought.

The alternative would have been to have a meltdown at work, and that kind of emotional display was something Samantha refused to allow herself. She'd always found it taxing when women cried in the workplace; in her mind it only gave men something to use against them in the fight to break through the glass ceiling. Men could raise their voices, shout, and throw tantrums, but the minute a woman cried at work she was considered weak and "not upper-management material."

It was complete and utter bullshit, but Samantha had learned long ago to play the game by the rules. Her tears were shed in private, or with Lola, but never in the presence of co-workers.

Sam eyed the two books she'd brought with her – one she'd had for a month now, and one she'd bought on impulse at the airport book stand. With a sigh, knowing she probably wasn't actually ready to quit her job, Samantha picked up the book that outlined the details of the new accounting software the company would be unrolling in the coming year, leaving the brightly colored romance novel untouched. Grabbing her notepad and pen, she bent to the book, forcing herself to focus lest she be left in the dust at the next meeting.

A movement from the beach pulled her eyes from the dreadfully boring chapter on converting spreadsheets and Sam paused to see what – or who – had interrupted her solitude.

As interruptions went, it was a doozy, Sam thought, glad that the sunglasses shaded her eyes and hoping her hat hid the fact that her mouth had dropped open. A man had pulled his kayak to shore down the beach, where Sam just now realized a house was all but hidden on a hill among swaying palm trees. Tanned skin rippled over lithe muscles as he hefted his kayak with an easy grace and put it on a small dock. Sam wondered if he worked for the owner of the villa. Tattered board shorts hung loosely from his hips and wraparound sunglasses shaded his eyes. Deep brown hair with just a kiss of sun at the tips had been left to grow a little long, and Samantha was astonished to find herself itching to run her hands through it. Now where had that thought come from? Sam was not one to fantasize; she hadn't even allowed herself to date since the disastrous end of her engagement. Her eyes slid to the cover of the romance novel on the table next to her, where a pirate readily embraced a woman whose bosom – it was always a heaving bosom in those novels – threatened to break free from her tightly laced bodice.

"Have you seen our dreamy neighbor?" A voice at her shoulder shocked Samantha out of her reverie; she'd been staring at the man like he was a piece of cake and she was on a diet.

"Excuse me?" Samantha asked, pulling her shoulders back and leveling a look at the woman who'd plopped into a lounge chair beside her.

"Him. The man you're looking at like you're a cat who wants to lap up a bowl of cream?" the woman said. All rounded curves and tumbling curls, she evoked a confident sensuality that Samantha could never muster even on her best days.

"I was most certainly not looking at him like I wanted to eat him," Samantha sputtered.

"Ignore her. Jolie would lap up every man she came across if she chose," Another woman slid into the chair on the other side, and Samantha turned to see another voluptuously beautiful woman smiling at her. Great, Samantha thought, refusing to look in the direction of the man who undoubtedly could see them. She was bookended by curvy knockouts and probably looked like a staid stick-in-the-mud tourist plastered in sunscreen and boring books.

"And every man would be lucky to have me if I let him," Jolie preened. She stretched languidly on the lounge, her screaming pink bikini leaving little to the imagination, her midnight curls tumbling everywhere.

"It's a blessing to mankind that you're more discerning, then, isn't it?" The woman on Sam's right was just as luscious in a simple white bikini, her blonde hair woven into intricate braids that reached almost to her waist.

"Don't act like you're so pure, Mirra. I saw you cuddling with that yacht captain from Antigua just last week," Jolie said, twirling a curl around her finger.

"I never said I was pure," Mirra demurred. "I merely told our guest here to ignore you as you're embarrassing her."

"I'm not –" Samantha protested, but Jolie had already sat up straight.

"Am I embarrassing you? I'm so sorry. My mouth gets ahead of me sometimes. A strength and a fault of mine, I suppose."

"Definitely a fault," Mirra said.

"It's not like you're perfect, Mirra." Jolie flounced back in her chair.

"I'm sorry… do you live here?" Samantha asked, flustered by their banter.

"See? You could have at least introduced yourself before you embarrassed her," Mirra said.

Samantha held up a hand to protest before letting it drop. There was no use trying to talk over these two, it seemed.

"Fine. I'm Jolie, evil sister to this pure-as-the-fallen-snow angel of a woman, Mirra, and we help our mother, Irma, run this guesthouse," Jolie said, sneering slightly at Mirra.

Sisters. That made sense of their casual bickering,

Sam thought as she shifted her gaze to Mirra, who rolled blue eyes the mirror of Irma's.

"I'm Samantha Jameson. I, uh, just booked in last-minute and plan to be here for a few weeks. It's nice to meet you both," Sam said, nodding at each of them with a smile.

"So, Samantha Jameson, what do you do in the real world?" Jolie asked, examining her manicure and relaxing back into her chair. With a resigned look at her books, Sam set them aside to talk, even though she was in no mood for company.

"I'm the senior accountant to Paradiso Hotel & Villas luxury portfolio," Samantha said.

Jolie whistled. "Faaancy," she said. "I've bet you've seen loads of beautiful places."

"And shopped in exotic boutiques," Mirra added with a sigh.

"And had your taste of even more exotic men," Jolie squealed. "Tell us everything."

Samantha found herself wishing she lived the life these women thought she did – in fact, what most people assumed she did. She wondered what it would be like to be so fearlessly confident. Briefly she envisioned herself strolling the boutiques in Morocco, haggling with the merchants, and taking a carefree lover with no strings attached. A giggle escaped before she could stop herself. It was so unlike her tightly wound and highly scheduled existence that the mere idea of even strolling anywhere with no agenda was a shock, let alone taking a lover on a whim.

"Oh, the woman has secrets," Jolie said, a wicked smile dancing on her face.

"No, I really don't," Samantha sighed. "I hate to burst your bubble, ladies, but my life has been more work than play. While I've seen some beautiful places, it's mainly been from the window of a conference room or from the backseat of a car on the way to or from the airport. I've had little time to explore."

"Well, that's a crying shame," Mirra said.

"I suppose it is, isn't it?" Samantha admitted.

"Not even one mysterious lover?" Jolie demanded.

"Hush now, Jolie. Not everyone wants to tell you their secrets, you know."

"I'm just asking," Jolie pouted.

"She's not ready to share. Let her settle in. Look at what she's reading, for god's sake." Mirra held up the accounting book and wrinkled her pert nose in distaste.

"Oh… that just breaks my heart," Jolie said, bringing a hand to her chest in dismay. "You're reading about software programs on this gorgeous beach when you've got eye candy like that in front of you?"

Helpless not to look where Jolie gestured, Sam peeked once more at the man on the beach who was now hosing off his kayak, whistling a merry tune as he worked.

"I'm trying to balance work and relaxation," Samantha said primly.

"I'd say you're not doing a very good job of it. Isn't vacation meant to be no work and all play?" Mirra asked sweetly.

"I don't know how not to work," Samantha heard herself say, and her fingers tightened around the arms of the chair as she realized it was true. She'd never really learned how to play – to just have fun – because she'd always been driven to succeed. Work wasn't meant to be joyful; it was a means to an end, as her family had instructed her over and over. Keep your nose to the grindstone, make partner in the law firm – or in her case, chief financial officer – and prove to everyone that you were the best and the brightest. The reward was the approval at cocktail parties as you one-upped everyone with your latest promotion, house purchase, or fancy vacation. It was a "keeping up with the Joneses" kind of lifestyle she'd been raised in, and Samantha hated every moment of it.

Though she'd never admit that to her family.

How could she? Both of her brothers were partners at the most prestigious law firm in town and her father still worked part-time, choosing only the most elite of the cases that crossed his desk. Her mother, in a move that had shocked and then delighted the family, had switched from handling divorce cases to maritime law, proclaiming that she was drawn to the sea. Her admittedly wild U-turn of practice choices had paid off, and now Elizabeth Jameson was one of the most sought-after maritime lawyers in the Great Lakes Region.

"Now that's a damn tragedy that you haven't learned how to have fun," Jolie drawled, scowling at Samantha. "What's life without a little fun?"

"I wouldn't really know," Samantha admitted. "I've been too busy to notice."

"Well, I say it's time for you to notice. Starting with that delicious man over there," Jolie purred.

Mirra shook her head in exasperation. "Jolie, not everyone is a man-eater. Don't push her toward Lucas," Mirra said, and the name seared its way to Sam's core.

Lucas.

What would it be like to be a Jolie? To stroll over to this Lucas and make him beg to be with her? The mere thought of it was so ludicrous that Samantha found herself laughing softly.

"She's not all boring. See?" Jolie held up the romance novel and Samantha immediately blushed at the couple writhing in ecstasy on the cover. "Our Samantha has a torrid side too."

"I most certainly do not. It was just an impulse buy at the airport," Sam insisted, heat creeping up her cheeks.

"The best kind of impulse buy," Mirra said, grabbing the book from Jolie. "I do love a delicious romance story, don't you? They're so much fun to read, and even more fun if you can act them out."

Act them out? Sam's mouth dropped open. She would never… her life didn't… no, *wasn't*… like a novel. Nothing interesting ever happened to Samantha, aside from her latest downfall at work. And there was certainly nothing romantic about losing the biggest promotion of her life.

"I've never read one, to be honest," Samantha said. "I have no idea what compelled me to buy that book."

"I'd say it's high time for you to read it, then," Jolie said, snatching Samantha's accounting book away from her. "I'll just hold onto this for a day or two while you settle into the book you should be reading."

"But… wait. You can't just take my stuff," Samantha called, but Jolie was already strolling away, completely unselfconscious in her scrap of a bikini.

"I would apologize for my sister once again, but I kind of have to agree with her on this one. If you've never even taken the time to read a romance novel, isn't this a great time to do it? Go on now… let yourself be free for a bit," Mirra said, her words gentle as she stood up and stretched, as confident as her sister in her tiny bikini and generous curves. Samantha found herself envying these women and their careless body confidence, though neither of them were remotely close to being what society declared a bikini body size must be. And they looked amazing for it, Samantha thought, wondering if she too could pull off wearing a bikini.

"What's with everyone here telling me to be free? I don't see anything wrong with having discipline," Samantha asked, using her boardroom voice for good measure.

"There's discipline and there's handcuffs. Which

one are you wearing?" Mirra asked, leaving before Samantha could even begin to reply.

What was with the people at this guesthouse? Samantha needed to have a few words with Lola immediately.

Sam pulled out her phone to send a strongly-worded text message to Lola, but was dismayed to see there was no internet service on the beach.

No internet and no work, Samantha grumbled, her gaze drawing back to Lucas, who was now sweeping the dock.

Now what was she supposed to do?

CHAPTER 5

"I can't believe you stole her book, Jolie," Mirra admonished Jolie as she propped herself on the kitchen counter, while Irma stirred a pot at the stove. The kitchen was the heart of their home, where the three always met to discuss the weighty topics of the world.

Designed in a Tuscan style, Irma had imported rough-cut stone to build the brick oven, the walls, and the backsplash that ran the length of the wall over the marble counters. Wood beams crisscrossed the ceiling, and a long table carved of mahogany dominated the room. Woven hangings in vibrant reds and blues decorated the room, and shelves full of bottles and tins lined one long stone wall. Open windows allowed the breeze to cut through the room, cooling the air.

"She needed a push to relax," Jolie shrugged, wrapping a brightly patterned sarong around her body and tying it behind her neck.

"You push too hard," Mirra said, leaning over to steal an oatmeal cookie from her mother's stash.

"I do not. She'll be forced to read her romance book now and maybe she'll consider actually having some fun on this vacation," Jolie grumbled, snatching the cookie from Mirra's hands and earning herself a glare.

"She doesn't know what fun is," Irma said. She leveled a look at Jolie, who hunched her shoulders and handed the cookie back to Mirra.

"And we'll show her. But you have to tone it down sometimes," Mirra argued.

"She's wounded, Jolie," Irma said simply, knowing both her daughters had a weakness for caring for all injured creatures.

"Ah… fine, I know, I know. I can't help but rush in sometimes. I want everyone to realize what a gift this life is and to savor every decadent moment of it," Jolie sighed, scooping her own cookie from the seahorse-shaped ceramic jar.

"Not everyone can learn that as quickly as you try to teach them," Mirra pointed out. "She seems completely bewildered that she's even here."

"Poor thing has never really taken a holiday," Irma said, lifting the spoon to her lips to sample her minestrone.

"And she's come alone, at that," Jolie said.

"I think she's used to traveling alone," Mirra said.

"For business, not for pleasure. I'm certain with business trips they keep you constantly busy, rushing from one meeting to the next. But this? This trip? It's a cry for help. The woman's on a verge of a breakdown. Tread carefully with her, you understand?" Irma said, covering the soup and setting it to simmer. Turning, she wiped her hands on the apron that protected her pretty sunset caftan.

"Should we show her who we are?" Mirra asked.

"Not now, sweet daughter of mine. Samantha's not yet ready to believe in us, let alone herself. You'll know when."

"Remember when the couple from Detroit saw you, Jolie? They about lost their minds," Mirra giggled.

"Okay, I'll admit they were the wrong ones to reveal myself to. But I couldn't help it. The man was so boring and the wife was aching to experience something different for once."

"Well, seeing a sea nymph in the ocean under the full moon certainly shook them up."

"You could've worn a top at least," Irma said.

Jolie shrugged. "You know I like going skyclad under a full moon."

"Good thing the man had drunk enough to believe it was too much rum that had him seeing naked women frolicking in the waves," Mirra laughed.

"The wife, though… she believed. A part of her did. I could read it in her soul." Jolie smiled, unfazed by their criticism. "A part of her wanted to come swim with me – to throw caution to the wind and dive naked beneath the waves."

"And so will this one," Irma said, her eyes crinkling at the corners again as she smiled at her two enchanting daughters. "Her spirt is there. It's buried deep, and she's wound tighter than a spring, but it's there. She needs time, Jolie. Frankly, she needs a friend."

Helpless against the urge to befriend even the most unhappy of creatures, Jolie's heart melted at the words. Crossing the room, she hugged Irma.

"We'll be her friends, right, Mirra?"

"Of course we will. Give her a little alone time to settle in and then we'll see if we can work our magick on her."

"That's my girls," Irma smiled.

CHAPTER 6

Despite her misgivings, Samantha found herself engrossed in the romance novel within a few chapters. After all, she needed to find out if the rakish Raphael claimed the stowaway princess as his lover, didn't she? She was so engrossed she'd barely looked up for quite some time, and was startled by a shadow falling over her legs.

"Ah, so the woman likes pirates, does she?" The man – Lucas, they had called him – smiled down at her. Sam could have buried her head in the sand.

"It's… research," she said, flipping the book onto the table with the cover side down. What was with this place? Why did everyone keep coming up to talk to her? Samantha thought it should be obvious – when a woman barricaded herself with books and an iPad on the beach, it was a clear sign she wanted to be left alone. Headphones, she decided, as she blushed up at the man who towered over her where she sat. Headphones should do the trick.

"Is that so? Do you work for a publishing house then?" Lucas said, leaning back and crossing his arms over his chest, now thankfully covered in a loosely-buttoned Hawaiian-style shirt.

"No," Sam said.

"Hmm, you're a writer?"

"Nope."

"Ah, then you must work for one of those sex shops that help men and women rekindle their pleasure in the bedroom."

"What? No!" Sam squealed, bringing her hands to her face to hide her embarrassment.

"Just teasing you," Lucas said, his tone gentle as he sat on the chair across from her. "My name's Lucas Mosteron."

"Hi, Lucas, my name is Samantha. I'm a senior portfolio manager at a luxury hotel line and I most certainly do not work at a sex shop." Samantha grimaced at the primness that laced her voice. Even to her she sounded like an old fuddy-duddy. It would have been the perfect time to throw on a new persona, maybe tell a few lies, and have some fun with someone she'd never see again. Too bad she couldn't bring herself to fake such bravado, Sam thought, wishing she had a bit of Jolie's sass in her.

"More's the pity," Lucas said, his teeth a flash of white in his face as he smiled at her. He was older than she'd assumed, probably at least five years older than her. Samantha found she didn't mind, though she had to admit her mind had briefly strayed to the idea of romancing a young college boy for the trip. Shocked at her train of thought, Sam glared at the romance novel. See? That was what those things did to you.

"I've never even been inside a shop like that," Samantha blurted, and then could have kicked herself. She'd barely met this man and was already telling him she'd never been in a sex shop? She might as well advertise herself as the boring accountant who blushed at the thought of reading a romance novel in public.

"Might I repeat myself? More's the pity." Lucas chuckled again, but his tone was easy, with no judgment.

Sam covered her face with her hands and shook her head back and forth.

"Can we start over? I'm totally embarrassed," she admitted. Lucas tilted his head to study her face, and once again, she was glad her sunglasses shaded her eyes.

"Hi Samantha, I'm Lucas. I was just going for a stroll on the beach and thought I'd stop to say hello to a pretty lady. I hope I'm not bothering you," Lucas said, all but oozing charm. Maybe she did want to lap him up like a bowl of cream, Sam mused, once again shocking herself with her thoughts.

"Hi Lucas, that's very sweet of you to stop and say hello. It's nice to meet you," she said. There, she sounded like a normal capable adult – which she was, most of the time and to everyone else who knew her in this world.

"Would you like to join me for a stroll on the beach?" Lucas asked, and Sam found herself wanting to say yes. Yes, she was carefree and easygoing enough to stroll with a stranger on the beach on this tiny speck of Siren Island in the middle of the Caribbean.

"I…" But Sam just couldn't quite bring herself to say it. She'd never been impulsive or frivolous, and she could just hear her parents lecturing her on personal safety. Strolling with a strange man on the beach? Not smart, Sam reminded herself; that's how people ended up in bathtubs with their kidneys missing.

Perhaps she should be a writer, Sam thought, with such gruesome images flashing through her brain.

"Maybe another time," Lucas said, gauging her response easily enough.

"Thank you, yes, maybe another time. Frankly, I'm exhausted and feel like I could sleep for a week," Sam said. She hoped she had let him down easily enough – so that maybe he really would come back another day to speak with her.

"You should do that then. It's good for the soul," Lucas said.

"I wouldn't really know," Sam said, and then wanted to shake her head at herself again.

"Long hours at work?" Lucas guessed.

"Brutal," Sam admitted, thinking of the weekly travel all over the world and all the time changes. Her body rarely was on a schedule, and sleep came only when she had some medicinal help. For the most part, she tried to ease into sleep with a Benadryl, but every once in a while – after days of barely sleeping – she'd pull out the big guns and use an Ambien. She hated the sleep she got those nights, but at the very least she was functional the next day.

"You'll rest easy here," Lucas said, rising and smiling down at her. "Siren Island has that effect on people. If you let it."

With that, Lucas turned and strolled away, gone before she knew what to say. When he reached the beach, he threw a smile at her over his shoulder. She found herself grinning back at him, wishing she'd had the courage to just stand up and walk along the beach with him.

"Maybe tomorrow," Sam promised herself as she gathered her things and slipped upstairs to her room. Ignoring the hunger pains that growled low in her stomach, she crawled into the bed, pulling the netting down to cocoon her in an ethereal nest.

In moments, she slid into sleep, still wearing her bathing suit, the romance book clutched in her fingers.

CHAPTER 7

Lucas wandered down the beach, his thoughts on the Laughing Mermaid's newest guest. They did tend to find the most interesting people, Lucas mused as he picked up a rock and skipped it into the ocean. He had become friends with the women over the years – never lovers, though Lucas had been tempted to cross that line a few times. Who wouldn't have? Irma, though older than him, had a carefree sexuality that appealed to him, while her daughters both packed a punch that had brought more than one man to his knees.

But Lucas had quickly surmised that sullying those waters wouldn't bode well for him, and had fallen into an easy friendship with his neighbors. It had proven to be a boon for him, as he had female companionship, homecooked meals, and relationship advice at his fingertips – oftentimes more than he needed, if truth be told. They did like to meddle, that was for sure. Lucas would be hard put to say no to those women, though, no matter what they asked of him.

It was best he didn't discuss the things he'd seen under the light of the full moon in the waters in front of their house.

As he knew well, the sea kept her own secrets.

It didn't surprise him that their newest guest had said no to a walk with him. Lucas usually kept to himself – he liked to socialize on his terms only – but something about the way the woman sat, totally entranced in her smutty novel, with an uptight energy about her, had made him stop and go over to say hello. He'd been delighted when she blushed over the book, even more so when she'd been flat-out embarrassed by his comment about the sex shop. Sure, he'd pushed the limits of what was proper in greeting someone, but he couldn't help testing her a bit.

Shit, Samantha was him ten years ago. A tightly-wound corporate stooge moments away from a break-down. He wouldn't be surprised if she had ended up here in the early stages of a crisis, much like he had.

He didn't miss it, that was for sure. After years of racing the clock, never enough hours in the day, living on coffee and a sugar-fueled diet, Lucas had finally and totally burnt out. His partners might have said he'd lost himself, but it wasn't until he left it all behind and retired to Siren Island that he'd really found himself.

Maybe he'd be able to help Samantha do the same, Lucas thought, as he tossed another rock into the water.

She sure was something to look at. A softly curved body tucked tidily into a neat one-piece suit, with all her beach amenities lined up in a row by her side. It had amused him to see her reading a romance novel. Perhaps she wasn't as prim and bottled-up as the image she presented to the world. There was something about her that made him want to unbutton her a bit at a time, starting with pulling the pins from her hair and working his way down that neat swimsuit inch by inch.

Lucas smiled again at the memory of the charming blush that had graced Samantha's face during their conversation.

Yes, Ms. Jameson might prove to be a very interesting diversion indeed.

CHAPTER 8

Samantha had rolled over at one point in the dim light of the early morning hours to the sound of her phone vibrating like mad in the tote she'd dropped at the foot of the bed. Groggy, she'd pulled it out to discover the internet was now working and that she had a torrent of incoming messages. Mainly from her disapproving family.

Where are you?

Why aren't you answering your phone?

Your brother said you failed to get the promotion.

How could you not make CFO?

Everybody is saying you left the country. Call me immediately.

If only you had worked harder, the CFO job would have been yours.

I hope the only reason you aren't answering your

phone is because you're wrapped in the arms of a handsome Caribbean hunk of a man.

The last text had been from Lola, and was the only one that had brought a smile to her face. She'd quickly responded to Lola with a promise to fill her in later, and had not only ignored but deleted the rest of the messages. Something about the act of deleting the messages from her family made her feel a little bit giddy and exhausted all in the same moment. Turning her phone off, she'd stripped out of her swimsuit and pulled the crisp white sheet over her naked body, luxuriating in the feel of cool cotton on her warm skin, and promptly fallen back to sleep.

She dreamed she could hear voices raised in song, dancing across the waves that crashed lazily on the shores beneath her balcony.

Sam blinked awake as a ray of sun moved across her face. Struggling to piece together where she was, Sam sat up and looked around the room. It finally registered – she was indeed still at the Laughing Mermaid on Siren Island in the middle of the Caribbean, and if she was guessing correctly based on the position of the sun, which hung low in the sky, she'd damn near slept for almost twenty-four hours. Both her need to use the bathroom and the angry grumbling of her stomach confirmed her suspicion that she'd slept longer than she ever had in her life, and Samantha dashed to the bathroom.

When she spied the decadent waterfall shower in the bathroom with the smooth white tiles and fluffy towels spread out so invitingly, Samantha decided food could be put off a moment longer. She dug in her bag for her toiletries and was soon surprised to find herself humming as she luxuriated in the shower.

Granted, she couldn't bring herself to sing in the shower yet – because, well, other guests might be able to hear and she would hate to disturb anyone. But it was hard not to be in a good mood after such a long sleep. Sam hummed her way through her shower and enjoyed slathering on some coconut citrus body lotion from a gorgeous blue pot next to the sink. Once she'd towel-dried her hair and slipped a simple black tank dress over her head, Sam gave in to the single-minded focus of finding food immediately.

Grabbing her purse, Sam opened the door and almost tripped over a tray that had been left at her door.

"I forgive you, Lola. This may be the best guest-house ever," Sam breathed in delight. She snatched up the tray of food and settled it on the small table on her balcony. She could have wept when she uncovered a still-warm tureen of minestrone, a basket of freshly baked bread, and a bowl of fruit. Without a thought to the calories the bread contained, Samantha ripped off a decadent chunk and dipped it in the soup, letting out a small sigh of contentment as she took the edge off the worst of the hunger.

Finally feeling like she could face the world a bit, Samantha dug out her phone and turned it on. Ignoring all the messages from work and her family, as they immediately made the food in her stomach turn, she called Lola.

"Girl, I've been wondering why I haven't heard from you," Lola's laughing voice sounded over the surprisingly clear connection.

"I'm sorry. I can't believe I'm saying this, but I just slept for almost twenty-four hours. Without any assistance. As in, down for the count," Sam said, crossing her legs and smiling as she watched a gull dip lazily over the crystal blue waves.

"Then you definitely needed it. Your body was telling you something. Are you okay?"

That was Lola, straight to the punch. Though Sam's family had always found Lola to be flighty, jumping from job to job, man to man, and traveling constantly, Samantha had always known she could count on Lola when it mattered. A part of her had secretly envied the carefree way in which Lola barreled through life, and had wished she could be a tad bit more easygoing than she was. Maybe not full-on Lola, as living Lola's life would probably send Samantha into a panic attack, but a dash of Lola's approach to life would be good for her.

"I am. Actually, I think I am. I haven't had much time to process anything, to be honest," Sam said, eying another piece of bread.

"I hope you finally leave that shithole job and take some time for yourself. I mean, you've got the savings for it. Why not take some time off?" Lola asked.

"Only you would describe my job as a shithole," Sam laughed.

"Well, it is. You fly all around the world but only get to see the inside of conference rooms, you never take your vacation time, and all the hard work you put in has been for what? To have your rightfully earned job handed to a suck-up of a coworker."

"He is a total kiss-ass, isn't he?"

"The worst kind," Lola agreed.

"I've taken three weeks here, you know. Which is longer than I've gone anywhere in pretty much ever," Samantha said.

"Take six months. That will really give you some time to sort yourself out," Lola said.

"I wish. It's not likely. I have to…"

"Have to what? Get back to a job that makes you unhappy? What exactly do you have to do?" Lola's words were blunt, and the truth of them hurt just a little.

"You're right, actually," Sam said, sadness creeping into her voice. "I don't really have anything to go back to, do I? That's kind of sad. No man. No cat. Not even a plant to water. God, what am I doing with my life?"

"Trying to play by your parents' rules?" Lola asked, her voice soft through the phone.

"I guess I just thought… if I finally got that promotion then – well, then I would be happy. That was the carrot at the end of the stick, you know?" Sam sighed, and ran one hand through her damp hair. She hadn't bothered to blowdry it in this heat, something else that was completely out of character for her. Usually she was perfectly coiffed at all times.

"When are you going to look at what you want for yourself and not what your family or society or the upper crust of our crappy city wants? What does it matter? When will you start living life for you?"

"I… I don't know. It's all I've ever known," Sam said, anxiety beginning to creep in once more. "The one time I tried to live for myself, aside from not going to law school, was when I dated Noah. And you know how well that turned out."

"It would have turned out better if you'd given him more of a chance. Introducing him to your family too soon was not a smart choice," Lola said. She'd been a fierce supporter of Noah, a struggling musician who worked at a bookstore to make ends meet. He'd been soulful, kind, and covered in tattoos. Sam had been swept away when she'd met him; Noah had looked at her like he could see her soul, not just what she presented to the world. But it hadn't taken long for her family to poison the relationship, and she'd been hurried into an engagement with Nathaniel, an up-and-coming attorney in her father's law firm.

Lola had hated him.

"What am I doing, Lola?" Sam whispered.

"I'd say you're having a well-deserved break. Take some time to think about what you want. You. Not your parents. Not your brothers. Not any of your colleagues at work. What makes you happy?"

"I don't know. I do like working with numbers; that was never the issue. I like how they all line up neatly," Sam said.

"That's fine. But can you work with numbers in another capacity? It doesn't always have to be the first choice that presents itself, you know."

"I've never even thought about it," Sam admitted. And she hadn't. She'd taken the best of the jobs offered to her after she'd graduated with top marks from university, and that had been it.

"Wouldn't now be a good time? I firmly believe that things happen for a reason. Maybe it isn't always clear to you why, but sometimes the universe throws a stumbling block in your path because you need to stop moving in the direction you're heading and take a damn look around you. And look at this! You've been busting your ass for years for this promotion and didn't get it. Why do you think that is?" Lola asked.

"Because I wasn't good enough." The words burned into Sam's gut. She rubbed a hand across her stomach and absently wondered if she was getting an ulcer.

"No, dummy. It's because it's not your destiny," Lola proclaimed.

"And you know what my destiny is?" Sam asked. It wouldn't surprise her. Lola was in touch with all sorts of psychics and tarot card readers and whatnot – she'd probably gotten a reading on Samantha at some point.

"No, I don't. But I know that you sound more alive during this phone call than you have in years, albeit a little sad and stressed. How many dinners have I had to sit through with you when you've just gotten back from someplace exotic like Majorca, only to have you bore me with the latest innovations in client reservation systems?"

"Ouch," Samantha said, biting her lip.

"Not ouch. I love you; I'll listen to you drone on about spreadsheets if that's what lights you up inside. But you weren't telling me about your job because you love it. You were telling me about it because it's all you know. Don't you want to know something different? Just for a little while, at least?"

"You know what, Lola? I think I do. I really think I might be ready for a change." When a little burst of excitement shot through her core, she realized that maybe Lola was right. And that panic that came rushing in on the cusp of the excitement? Well, she'd just try to pretend that didn't exist. At least for the next three weeks.

Maybe coming to Siren Island had been the best decision she'd made in a long time.

"Thatta girl. Now don't call me again until you've got some juicy gossip. Nothing to do with spreadsheets. Oh, and ignore all text messages from your parents and work."

"I have to let them know I'm safe," Samantha said automatically.

"So tell them you're alive, that you're taking a well-deserved vacation, and then shut your phone off. That's an order."

"Yes, ma'am."

CHAPTER 9

She'd need a car.

Samantha berated herself for not having thought to reserve one, but she was used to traveling to more metropolitan places that always had taxis available. How was she going to get around this island if she didn't have a car? Although, now that she thought about it, where was she even going to go? It was a decidedly unnerving experience to have no agenda whatsoever. She drummed her fingers nervously on the table as she searched through the guidebook Irma had left for her.

"There. Car rental."

Grateful for her international phone plan, Samantha placed the call, and was even happier to hear they offered a car delivery service. Better and better.

"Now, where am I going?"

Seeing as how it was already late afternoon, Samantha decided on just a quick trip to the grocery store for a few essentials, a bottle of wine, and a small look at the town to get her bearings. Then she'd hustle back and catch the sunset and read more of her smutty romance novel. There, that's something Lola would do, Sam thought. Well, Lola would probably go out and live the smutty romance novel, but Sam was taking baby steps here. It took everything in her power not to switch on her phone and check for work emails. She'd always been readily available for work, and she could only imagine the fit they were having with their emails getting zero response.

"You're taking a holiday from work, Samantha Jameson. Normal people can turn off their work and go on a vacation. They even put a vacation responder on their email and the rest of the world just has to deal. Life goes on. The company will be fine without you," Sam lectured herself as she went downstairs to wait for the car delivery.

"The company will most certainly be fine without you," Jolie said from the base of the stairs, giving Sam a jolt. She'd been so stuck in her head that she hadn't even noticed the woman – looking as radiant as yesterday in a brilliant blue caftan with her midnight hair pulled back in twists and curls.

"Oh, I didn't mean to talk out loud," Samantha said, feeling heat creep across her face. Would she be constantly unnerved around these people?

"No bother. We all talk to ourselves. How was your rest?" Jolie asked, propping a hip on the banister and smiling at Sam in a friendly manner. She seemed to have lost a bit of her edge from yesterday, and Sam briefly wondered if Mirra had lectured her.

Be nice to the crazy woman. She's about to have a breakdown.

"I don't think I've ever slept so long in my life. I can't believe I've missed almost a full day of vacation," Sam apologized, tugging the strap of her bag onto her shoulder.

Jolie tilted her head and studied Samantha through piercing blue eyes that seemed to see straight into her soul.

"Why would you apologize for sleeping? We all need sleep," Jolie asked, her tone light.

"Because it seems a wasteful way to spend an entire day – in paradise, no less. I should be doing…" Sam's voice trailed off. It felt uncomfortable to not have an itinerary, or even a hint of an idea of what she should be doing with her time.

"Doing what?"

"Uh, I suppose I don't know. I'm used to being highly scheduled in all aspects of my life," Sam admitted.

"Isn't a holiday meant to be just that – a holiday? A break from routine?" Jolie asked, twirling a long chain that hung between her breasts. Samantha wanted to smile at the sparkly mermaid pendant at the end of the chain.

"So I've been told," Samantha murmured, giving Jolie a sheepish smile.

"I think you're doing a lovely job of holidaying," Jolie twinkled at her, all smiles and good cheer. "You've thrown your schedule out the window, slept for twenty-four hours, and I have to say you look decidedly better for it. You were a bit scary when you arrived."

"Jolie," Mirra warned from the doorway. Surprised, Sam realized she must have been standing there for a while.

"What? Well, she did. All pale and tense. Look at her now. She's got some color in her cheeks, the shadows aren't so dark under her eyes, and she seems more relaxed. I'd say it did her a world of good," Jolie said, rolling her eyes at her sister.

"Please excuse Jolie, she's not always the best with human – I mean, the most tactful with people." Mirra seemed to catch herself, and the sisters exchanged a look that put Sam's senses on alert.

"I'm complimenting the woman, aren't I? How is that not tactful?" Jolie grumbled, then beamed as a dusty two-seater pickup truck rolled to a stop in front of the villa. "See? Look at that. She's even gone and rented herself a truck. I'd say our Samantha is doing just fine for herself."

Jolie raced outside in a flurry of blue silk and streaming curls, and Sam watched as a slack-jawed teenager nodded enthusiastically at whatever she was saying to him. Sam commiserated with the boy: Jolie was a force of nature.

"There now, I've got you all sorted. Terry's promised you'll get the local discount rate, and he's even leaving a local cellphone in the car in case you need help. You're a doll, Terry, have I told you that?"

The boy blushed and nodded, his brown eyes full of devotion for Jolie. A jaunty beep sounded and Terry waved as a similarly run-down island pick-up truck sailed by and scooped him up. In moments, they were gone and Samantha stood gaping at the truck.

"Don't I have to sign any papers?"

"Nah, they know where to find us if there's any issues." Jolie waved it away and then smiled at Samantha.

"Where are you headed? Do you need directions?" Mirra asked.

"Um, I'm thinking just a grocery store or market for some fruit and a bottle of wine. Maybe take a peek at the town. Is there a town?"

The sisters both broke into laughter at that. The sound was a song all its own and birds began to sing in response in the trees. Shading her eyes, Sam looked up to see two bright green birds with brilliant yellow shoulders squawking in the branches of the plumeria tree above them.

"They aren't the ones singing," Mirra said, wiggling her fingers at the parrots. "They sure are pretty, aren't they? Couldn't carry a tune if their life depended on it, though."

One of the birds let out a squawk of indignation, surprising a chuckle from Samantha. It just looked so… annoyed at Mirra's words, fluffing its feathers up and dancing its head up and down.

"We all must play to our strengths, lovies, you know that." Mirra blew a kiss to the birds and they both bounced their heads in delight.

"They really are stunning," Samantha said, enjoying their brilliant colors.

"See, darlings? She thinks you're pretty too. Now don't fuss too much about not being able to sing. We make do with what we have," Mirra said, and the birds flew off, seemingly content with her words.

Sam almost shook her head at herself. Here she was thinking parrots had personalities and could understand what they were saying. Maybe she was slowly going off the deep end.

"The town, all four blocks of it, is not far from here. Just follow this dirt road until it becomes paved. It'll take you past the grocery store and various restaurants or huts. There are a few stands on the side of the road that sell fruit, and delicious juices as well," Jolie said.

"Great, sounds good. I should be back in not too long. If I don't get lost, that is," Sam said, trying to sound more confident than she felt. She rounded the truck and plopped into the driver's seat, noting the lack of leather seats and –

were those actual manual window cranks? She wondered what year the car was made. Her eyes tracked to the controls as a quick spurt of panic hit her, but it was quickly put to rest when she saw the air conditioning switch.

"There's really one main road. On your way back, look for the mermaid statue tucked in the trees. Turn left after it, and you'll find us again. If not, call for help."

"Will do." Samantha smiled her thanks as the girls went inside.

It was only then that the panic hit like a bag of bricks to her head.

"Help!"

Jolie scampered back out with Mirra at her heels.

"What's wrong, darling?"

"I can't… this is… I can't drive this." Sam gestured helplessly at the stick shift transmission.

The sisters slid each other a look, and then turned back to Sam. She knew what they were thinking – "Americans" – but she didn't care. Automatic was easier to drive and that was that.

"Didn't your daddy ever teach you to drive a manual?" Jolie asked, leaning in the window.

"We had a few lessons years ago before giving up. There was that one time I drove a stick in Tasmania, but that was out of sheer necessity."

"See? You'll pick it right back up. Let me help," Jolie said, and hopped into the dusty front seat, unconcerned about her pretty blue caftan getting dirty. Samantha wondered if dust was just something everyone on the island accepted, as it seemed to be everywhere.

"I'm not so sure about this," Sam said anxiously.

"Do you remember the basics?" Jolie asked.

"It's an H, right?"

"Yup, the gears are set up in a standard H. To change gears, you'll need to press the clutch in."

Sam looked down at the third pedal on the floor-board, and gingerly found it with her foot.

"Maybe I should just get another car," Samantha said, throwing Jolie a desperate glance.

"Honey, they're all manual. Good luck finding an automatic on island, unless someone shipped it in for private use. You'll be fine. We're used to tourists stalling. The locals do a good job of not crowding your car at stops or hills."

"Hills…" Samantha gulped, realizing she simultaneously didn't want to have to drive to buy that bottle of wine, and wanted it more than ever.

"It's no worries. You'll get on just fine. Go on now, turn it on." Jolie patted the truck like a lover and Samantha almost whimpered.

She only had herself to blame for this.

CHAPTER 10

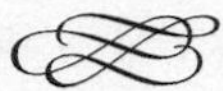

She bought caftans. And sarongs. And a long dangly necklace with stones the color of the sea.

"This would be lovely on you." The shop owner, spying a mark as soon as Samantha had stepped in the door, a sheen of sweat covering her from the panic of stalling four times and trying to find a parking spot, had quickly ushered her to stand under the air conditioner. She chatted easily with Samantha and finally, once the cool air had calmed her nerves a bit, Samantha had looked weakly around to discover a shop full of brightly colored fabrics – flowing dresses, elegant caftans, and easy beach pants. There wasn't a black dress to be seen.

"I… I couldn't wear that," Samantha gulped, staring at the siren-red bikini the woman held before her.

"It comes with a matching wrap. See how pretty it

would be with your skin tone?" The woman, her face creased in a smile, held the suit up in front of Samantha.

"It's just that… I don't know if I can wear a bikini," Samantha said, glancing down at her body and back at the suit.

"And why not? Every woman should own a pretty suit to make a man's head turn." The store owner laughed, a big booming laugh that suggested she'd made more than one man's head turn in her time.

"That's… highly unlikely with me," Samantha said and then began internally berating herself. Why was she putting herself down? Men often approached her – though unfortunately it was usually in the work environment and at highly inappropriate times. Perhaps if she did more than just work all the time she'd be approached elsewhere, Samantha could all but hear Lola's chiding voice say in her head.

"Ah, you Americans are so uptight with your bodies. Relax, enjoy, live your life. Nobody on the island will judge you – only you." With that, Samantha was pressed behind a fitting curtain, suit in hand.

Samantha held the suit up in front of herself, because the last thing she was going to do was peel off her sweat-soaked sundress and wrench her body into a bathing suit, rolling the material up her sticky skin. Standing there, she studied herself, seeing now how the black of her simple tank dress washed her out – highlighting those shadows beneath her eyes that she habitually covered but barely paid attention to, so consistently did they mar her skin. The red stood out like a flame against the black of her dress and as Sam held the wrap close to her skin she saw it did seem to warm her. She missed wearing red, she realized. Why had she limited her wardrobe to a sea of black and muted colors? Suddenly hating the dress she wore, Sam poked her head out of the curtain.

"Pick out a dress for me, please. In red."

That was how Samantha found herself wandering back to her car, two hefty shopping bags in hand, one filled to the brim with brightly colored fabrics – none of which would be appropriate for her frigidly cold offices in the States – and the other with fruit, cheese, a baguette, and several bottles of wine. Pleased with her purchases, Samantha surprised herself once more by humming her way back to the truck and depositing the packages on the dusty front seat.

"Now, drive this truck like an island girl," Samantha ordered herself and smiled at a man who nodded at her from across the street. It wasn't the first greeting she'd received since she'd left the shop wearing her new red dress – a maxi dress that was cut low over her breasts and had bright blue pom-poms at the hem. It was more daring and, at the same time, more freeing than she would usually have chosen, but since nobody knew her here, she decided she just didn't care.

The shop owner had explained that islanders typically didn't wear black, as the mosquitos were attracted to it. Not to mention the midday heat. Samantha had looked around as she'd wandered the town and saw that the woman was right. Bright colors and light pants and dresses were typical – not a black business suit to be seen. Samantha wondered what a life like this would be like. Moseying into town each morning to open a shop, closing for a long lunch, leaving at five on the dot to have a rum on the beach and watch the sun set over the stunning waters that hugged the coastline.

Mirra had been right. The town really was only about four blocks long, and the main thoroughfare consisted of brightly colored buildings that housed a variety of businesses – a multi-shop that seemed to sell everything from hand soap to laminate flooring; tourist shops with all the expected t-shirts screaming 'Siren Island' in neon colors; and a couple of bar restaurants where people nursed their drinks and played dominoes in the lazy afternoon sun.

Maybe one of these days Sam would feel comfortable enough to drive down and have a bite to eat on her own at one of the restaurants – the one with barrel tables and swings for seats looked particularly fun. A giggle escaped as she thought about herself, coconut drink in hand, sending a picture to Lola of her in a swing and her bright red dress. Her friend would be ecstatic.

But for now, Samantha needed to tackle the drive home. Traumatized from her drive earlier, she turned the key and gingerly let up on the clutch as she pressed down the gas – then jerked back into her seat as the car slammed to a stop and died.

The man across the street chuckled.

Sweat broke out her forehead and Samantha glared at the air conditioner, which limply fanned her with little puffs of barely-cooled air.

"Okay, lovey," Samantha cooed to the truck like Jolie had, "we can do this together."

Once more she eased off the clutch and pressed the accelerator.

"Damn it!" Samantha smacked the steering wheel, pointedly ignoring the chuckling man across the street.

Three tries and several inventive curses later, Sam shot into the street, narrowly missing an oncoming car, and coolly acknowledged the man who now sent her an approving nod. Sweat dripped down her back and Sam wondered if sweat stains would show through this fabric. See? If she'd been wearing black, nobody would see her sweat.

She gripped the wheel more tightly as she approached a series of hills, the pavement – well, if it could be called paved, with all the potholes – turning to dirt. Grinding the gears, Sam shifted and the car lunged forward, limping its way up the hill.

"Come on, baby, come on. You've got this," Sam chanted, gingerly applying more gas as she crested the top of the second hill. She was now seriously dripping in sweat and anxiety crawled at her throat, but then she saw the mermaid statue tucked at the base of a cheerful palm tree.

"Yes!" Sam shouted and steered the truck left onto

the small dirt lane, just as three goats launched themselves from where they'd been concealed in the bushes. A scream tore from Samantha's throat as she heard the distinctive ding of metal hitting a hoof or a horn, she wasn't sure what, and the truck died on the spot because she'd slammed on the brakes, completely forgetting to downshift.

Putting her head on the steering wheel, she wept.

CHAPTER 11

"Hey… hey now. Miss Samantha Jameson, hey… can you look up at me? Are you all right then?"

Samantha closed her eyes and shook her head back and forth. The majority of her crying fit had passed, but her embarrassment at hearing Lucas's voice threatened to bring it back on.

"Are you injured? Should I go for a doctor?"

He was already opening the door and running his hands gently over her body. For a moment Samantha was too shocked at his touch to move, a delicious heat seeming to follow his hands as they trailed down her legs. Then, batting his hands weakly away, she leaned back in the seat and met his eyes.

"Oh, honey. Having a bad day?" Lucas asked. He'd shoved his sunglasses up on his head and for the first time she could see his eyes, a dusky yellowish-green, now filled with concern for her.

"I… I hit a goat!" Samantha wailed and covered her face with her hands.

"Shhh, come here. Here, let's get you out of this truck," Lucas said, neatly unsnapping her safety belt and tugging her from the truck. Samantha stood on wobbly legs, turning away from the front of the car. She couldn't bring herself to look – she couldn't bear it.

"I heard it. It dinged. I heard it hit the front," Samantha said, her eyes filling again as Lucas pulled her into his arms, pressing her facc to his chest. She breathed in the scent of soap and sea air, wanting to snuggle against him until she could stand on her own again.

"Was it three goats? A group of three?" Lucas murmured, his lips by her ear.

"Oh no… I hit all three of them?" Samantha dragged in a breath. This was what happened when she went adventuring. Innocent creatures died. She should have known better.

"Sweetheart, look," Lucas said, turning her by the shoulders to point into the bushes on the far side of the road. There, three goats munched on the leaves of a tree – though one did turn and look angrily back at her. Or at least that's what it felt like.

"They're safe," Samantha breathed.

"These goats are quicker than they look. This isn't their first time playing dodge with island trucks. They'll be just fine. See? No blood," Lucas said, stepping away from her to check the front of the truck. She missed his presence instantly, and found herself wanting to be surrounded by his arms again. There was something about him that seemed safe to her in this moment. He was just so big and strong… and capable.

Something she was trying to prove that *she* was, with this trip, she reminded herself. A capable adult who'd taken herself off on an adventure. She certainly shouldn't be in a puddle of tears after not killing a goat.

"Thank you. I'm sorry for the tears. God… I've never been much of a crier. But something about driving a stick shift today just really put me out of my element," Samantha said.

Lucas laughed, walking back to put his hands on her shoulders. "Driving in a new country can be daunting for anyone. And manual cars bring their own particular challenges. You should be proud of yourself for giving it a go," Lucas said as he glanced into the truck. "Did some shopping, I see?"

"I did. I stumbled into a boutique in a ball of anxiety after parking in what I'm certain wasn't a legal parking spot, and before I knew it this shop owner had my hands full of dresses that I most certainly do not need."

"Charlene. She's great. I'd say she's done you a service, if she picked out the dress you're wearing. It's stunning on you," Lucas said, his gaze sliding down her body, causing warm little trills of excitement to pull long and low inside of her at his look.

"Ahhh, thank you, but you don't have to say that." Samantha blushed, knowing she probably looked a mess between her crying jag and the sweat running down her back. She'd never been one to cry pretty. It had always amazed her how the women in the movies could blink out tears, looking all doe-eyed, not a hair out of place when they cried. When she did cry – which was not often, for this exact reason, among others – she looked more like a toddler with the flu. Or several strains of flu.

"Why? I call it like I see it," Lucas said, leaning a hip against the truck as he studied her.

"I'm sure I look like a cat that's been just tossed in a bath. It's not the best look for me."

"Obviously I'd rather see you smiling," Lucas said, "but that certainly doesn't change the fact that red's your color and that's a mighty fine dress Miss Charlene picked out for you."

Oooookay. Samantha realized the man just might really be flirting with her. Even if she likely had slobber on her chin.

"Thank you, that's very kind of you." Samantha looked around herself, realizing they were still in the middle of the road. "Shouldn't I move this truck? I'm sure to be blocking traffic." She looked at the truck with distaste, not wanting to try and start it again. Her patience was shattered for the day.

"How about this? I'll drive the truck back if you share a bottle of that wine I see sticking out of the bag there."

It made her feel good, she realized, to have a man flirt with her even after she'd just sobbed in his arms like a sodden mess of a crazy woman.

"You have yourself a deal. I was ready to put it in neutral and push it back," Samantha said and then looked to where his 4-Runner was parked. "Aren't you on your way somewhere though?"

"No place in particular to be tonight. I was going to head down to the market and pick up a few bits to go with my wine for sunset is all."

"I have some bits," Samantha blurted out.

Lucas's slow smile caused heat to cover her face. "You most certainly do," he said, smiling appreciatively and overselling his leer so she knew he was joking.

"Oh my gosh, stop it," Samantha laughed, smacking him lightly on the shoulder as she clambered into the passenger seat next to him.

"What? I was looking at that cheese you have in there. It's my favorite," Lucas nodded at the bag she'd pulled onto her lap. Samantha found herself chuckling as he shifted smoothly into gear and delivered them neatly to the front door of the Laughing Mermaid.

"I'll meet you in the garden in fifteen or so?"

"Sounds good," Samantha said. It was enough time for her to try and freshen up, but not enough to let her anxiety overtake her.

"And Sam?"

"Yes?" Samantha said, turning at the door to the villa.

"Keep the dress. I like it," Lucas gestured to red dress and winked before he whistled his way back up the dirt road.

Okay, so maybe there was enough time for her anxiety to kick in. Samantha groaned and raced upstairs, already afraid to look in the mirror.

It didn't matter, she told herself.

After this vacation, she'd never see this man again.

CHAPTER 12

Samantha knocked at the kitchen door, fidgeting nervously with the strand of sea-colored beads she'd added to her outfit. They nestled coolly between her breasts, making her feel a little decadent.

"Samantha, don't you look lovely," Irma commented as she slid open the old-world barn door on its rollers.

"Thank you. I bought this dress today," Samantha said, smiling at Irma and then gasping at the kitchen behind her. "Your property is just perfect. In every aspect. This kitchen is so… homey."

"Thank you. I always feel the heart of the home is in the kitchen. Would you like to come in?" Irma asked. "I'm just making some sweets. I had a hankering for coconut chocolate bars."

"Oh, I don't want to bother you. It's just, well, I have a – well, it's not a date. It's just a thing. A drink.

Between friends, that is. Something for the cheese is what I wanted to see if you had. It's not a date. He helped me, you see. I hit a goat." Samantha closed her eyes and drew in a breath. Get your shit together, woman, she ordered herself.

Irma's eyes widened and then she threw back her head and laughed, her bracelets jangling at her wrists.

"Let me see if I've got this straight. You're having a drink – with Lucas, I presume?"

"Yes – how did you know? Is that what he does? Hits on every woman who stays here?" Samantha narrowed her eyes at Irma, twisting the handle of the bag between her fingers.

"He most certainly does not. Our Lucas mostly keeps to himself. We've been hoping he'd find someone," Irma said, reaching up to open a gleaming wood cupboard door.

"Oh. I'm not someone. I'm just. It's not…" Samantha sighed. "God, this is annoying. When did I become such a stuttering mess?"

"I'm sure it's just a passing thing. It seems like you've got a lot going on." Irma slid a cheese board onto the lovely weathered-stone island and waved her over. "Come, let's put the board together."

"I'm much more confident in real life," Samantha said, pulling out the goodies she'd gotten at the market. Mango, a few cheese selections, the baguette, sugared almonds, and the wine.

"And this isn't real life?" Irma laughed.

"Not for me it's not. Maybe for you," Samantha said, unwrapping a crumbly blue cheese.

"It could be for you too. Did you ever think that the life you're living back home is your fake life and this is really you?"

"An anxious crying mess?" Samantha raised an eyebrow at Irma. "You're not exactly selling me here."

"That's not what I'm seeing." Irma smiled and pulled out two wine glasses with delicate mermaids etched on the glass. "I see a woman who was brave enough to travel on her own to another country – one that she's never been to; who forced herself to drive a car she doesn't know how to operate; and who still went out and bought herself a pretty dress. On top of it, she's landed herself a hot date. I'd say you're doing just fine."

"What about the goat?" Samantha shot back, but she enjoyed hearing Irma's perception of her. Her words seemed to soothe the knot of anxiety that wrapped around her stomach like a coiling snake.

"Ah, that's island life. We've all bumped a goat here and there. They learn quickly to move faster."

Samantha laughed the entire way to the garden.

CHAPTER 13

"That's what I like to see – a laughing woman." Lucas stood from where he'd been sitting by the water in a low-slung chair with bright orange cushions. The garden here was more like a fairy garden, Samantha thought, with little secret spots tucked away between palm trees and rocks. Lucas had chosen two chairs tucked into the trees with a small table between them. He hurried over to help her with the board and glasses.

"Is that a plumeria tree?" Samantha asked, stopping to sniff a bloom before she sat.

"Frangipani, or jasmine as you probably know it."

"It smells divine," Samantha said, lowering herself into the chair with a smile as she looked at the sun hanging low in the sky. "This is a knockout view."

"Isn't it just? I never tire of it," Lucas agreed, and

bent to pick up a small bowl at his feet. "I made you something."

"Made me something? When did you have time for that?" Sam asked, then brought her hand to her heart when he lifted out a small garland of jasmine flowers.

"Just now. See how the tree drops her blooms? It's quite easy to slide a thread through the heart of them and soon enough you have a pretty crown fit for a queen," Lucas said, handing her the white flowers with soft yellow centers. Sam breathed deeply of their delicious fragrance before placing it lightly on her head, immediately feeling both foolish and unexpectedly thrilled at wearing a flower crown.

Didn't every woman want to wear a crown once in her life?

"How do I look?" Samantha said, laughing at him from under her flowers. "Like a queen?"

Lucas framed his fingers in a rectangle, like an artist capturing the image in his mind to paint later. "You look like you're blooming," he said softly, his gaze appreciative.

Sam smiled. If it really was time for her to bloom, perhaps this wasn't such a bad place to do it. Though at thirty-eight years of age, she should have already bloomed, her inner critic admonished. Or was that her mother's voice? Hard to tell, these days, and if she thought too hard about it the old resentful ache would burn through her stomach.

"Uh-oh. You went from smiling to looking slightly

pained. Did I say something to distress you?" Lucas asked, his handsome face creasing with worry.

"No, you did not. My own demons, I suppose." Samantha waved it away with a flick of her wrist. "Should we try this wine?"

"Of course." Lucas neatly opened the bottle. "Care to share more about those demons?"

Samantha opened her mouth to let it all pour out – the job, the stress, the deep-rooted guilt and anger that seemed to be intertwined with never living up to her family's expectations, her loneliness… and then looked around herself. The sun dropped low to the horizon, casting her rays in a golden-red net across the gentle water, and Sam realized that she absolutely did not want to share. Not yet, or at least not now. This was a moment meant to just be – no discussion of yesterdays gone, and none of future worries on the horizon.

"Frankly, no, I don't. It all seems so far away when I'm sitting here, looking at this beauty," Samantha said, accepting a glass of wine and gesturing out to the water.

"The ocean does have that effect on you," Lucas said, settling back and stretching long legs out in front of him to cross his feet at the ankles. Samantha turned to look over at him. Not only did he carry an air of confidence with him, but he just seemed so… relaxed. In fact, a lot of people on the island did. She wondered if that was what happened when you moved to an island – worries just melted away.

"Have you been here long?" Samantha asked. She

wanted to know all the details about this handsome man next to her – most importantly, why was he still single?

"Off and on for ten years or so. Initially it was just to visit, but then I kept returning here on holiday. Eventually, I knew it was time for a change. And so I packed my bags, and here I am." Lucas smiled at her, and Samantha found herself smiling right back, even though he hadn't given her any of the gritty details she secretly craved. What did he do for a living? How was he making money on the island? Did he rent the villa on the beach? Own it? Had he ever married? Were there kids? If Lola were here, she'd have dug out the details in a casual manner over the course of a glass of wine, but Samantha had never had the easy conversational prowess that Lola did.

"It must have been a good move for you. You appear quite content," Samantha said, sampling a bit of the cheese.

"I am, for the most part. I'd say island living presents its own unique set of challenges. But so do most places. I think with anything in life you trade certain stresses for others. For example, I no longer have to deal with shoveling snow. However, I do have to deal with cockroaches wandering their way into the bedroom once in a while."

"Ewww," Samantha breathed, and Lucas laughed.

"See? Different stressors. I'll still take the occasional bug over a Chicago winter."

"I don't blame you. Do you miss the seasons?"

"I thought I would, but not much. Sometimes I miss being cold," Lucas admitted.

Samantha rolled her eyes at him. "Miss being cold? Come on."

"No, really!" Lucas laughed at her. "It's so warm here all year long. Granted, we get a rainy season and there are times it's chilly. But I honestly miss being cold – as in, wearing jeans and a cozy sweater, stoking a fire and curling up in a heavy blanket while the snow falls outside. I always loved watching the snow fall. I just hated shoveling it or commuting in it."

"That ugly grey sleety slushy snow," Samantha agreed.

"That's been tromped all over and turned to a sheet of ice you can't see under the fresh snow," Lucas said.

"Which you inevitably fall on in front of people." Samantha smiled.

"Always."

"So now… Siren Island. A long way from the cold winters on the shores of Lake Michigan. I like the name of the island. Is that because it calls to you?" Sam asked. She was surprised to see she'd already finished her glass of wine.

Lucas smoothly refilled her drink, then leaned back in his chair once more, turning his head so that his eyes met hers. Her mind flashed back to when she'd been cradled in his arms earlier. Though he wore a loose linen shirt, Samantha had been up close and personal with the muscles beneath it.

"The official explanation is that sailors used to claim they could hear sirens singing over the waves," Lucas said, gesturing toward the end of the island where a rocky outcropping of cliffs jutted proudly into the sea.

"I swear I heard singing last night – but it was also in the middle of my almost twenty-four hours of sleep so I can't exactly vouch for that," Samantha laughed.

"A whole day of sleep? You most certainly did need it then," Lucas said. "And you might have heard singing."

"Really?" Samantha asked, snagging a sugared almond, intrigued.

"Well, at least what they say is singing. Up by the cliffs are long narrow caverns. When the tides come in or out, the rush of the water creates an echo-like sound that often can be mistaken for singing."

"No way," Samantha said. "That's so interesting. I've never heard of anything like that. I wonder how the caves are made so that it sounds like songs. Can visitors go there? Does it really sound like singing? Have you heard it?"

"Well, that's the official explanation, as I said. To answer your questions – no, you aren't supposed to go there. Yes, I have heard it, and I do believe it sounds like singing. But I'm more apt to believe the local lore than the official explanation."

“The locals don’t believe in the caverns?” Sam asked, wondering why they wouldn’t believe in the caves when they could easily see them in the cliffs.

“The locals believe in the sirens.”

CHAPTER 14

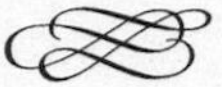

"Ohhhh," Samantha said. "Tell me, tell me."

Lucas laughed and raised the bottle to top their glasses off.

"Settle in, pretty lady, as I've got quite a story for you," Lucas said.

Samantha sighed in delight, leaning back in her chair to look out over the horizon. The sun had already sunk far below it, but the pink rays still kissed the wisps of clouds that danced across the sky over the sea.

"A couple hundred years ago, this island was just a small fishing village. Visits from larger European ships were rare, but vessels from other local islands would often make their way over for trading," Lucas said, pointing to the sky, where the first star popped into view. "The islanders found they enjoyed these visits from those on neighboring islands, and soon new routes were proposed – for both business and pleasure. You see, island life can be a little slow. Visitors always brought with them some excitement – or danger, but either way, it was something new and different."

"I'm sure," Samantha said.

"Plus, the villagers would fall in love or yearn to see other lands and so on, so more shipping and trading routes were mapped and the island population began to grow a bit. Which meant more sailors trying to navigate the treacherous waters around the island – and with that came stories. Of things seen in the water, and spoken of in hushed whispers."

"Mermaids," Samantha breathed, sipping her wine and looking out at the cliffs in the dim light.

"Mermaids. Or sirens. One and the same, though different cultures have their own derivatives of each."

Samantha nodded. "Sure. Some are evil, some are good, some are half-seal like the Selkies."

"Ah, the woman does read some lore," Lucas smiled, his eyes crinkling deeply in the corners.

"It's hard not to find mermaids enchanting. It's probably the main reason I took my friend's suggestion and booked this villa – for the name alone."

"I feel like every woman wants to be a mermaid, or at the very least has some mermaid essence in her," Lucas said, turning to study her.

"I haven't found mine yet, if that's what you're looking for." Samantha raised an eyebrow at him.

"Hmmm. Maybe you just don't see what I'm seeing," Lucas said softly, and Samantha blushed into her wine, biting back a smile of delight. Even if it was meaningless flirting – what did it matter? It was never bad to make someone feel good about themselves.

"Well, as I was saying, the fishermen began to report seeing a woman way out in the waves, singing to the moon. Or nestled on the rocks, half naked and combing out her hair. Of course, most of this was met with great doubt and simply dismissed. And so the stories became just that – stories to be talked about over a fire here and there, but with most believing there to be little truth to them."

"Still an interesting diversion," Samantha commented.

"Naturally. One time they had planned all month for a festival to honor the sea and how she nurtured their lives, providing fish and seaweed and so on. Many boats came from many islands – the fire was big, the dancing carefree, and a full moon rose that night. Now, one of the most handsome men in the village was a young fisherman named Nalachi. He spent his days fishing and his nights tending to his family, particularly his ailing mother. Though many a pretty woman approached him, Nalachi wasn't interested – he would rather dream up stories and learn what lay over the next horizon than try to bed one of the local maidens."

"A dreamer, our Nalachi," Samantha murmured.

"Correct, a dreamer he was. So when a woman stepped into the festival – a woman he'd never seen before – and caused his heart to skip a beat, he knew he had to make his way to her. No woman had ever caught his eye, or his imagination, like this one did. She was a goddess, throwing herself into the dancing, the firelight playing in her curls, her dress oddly woven from shells and palm leaves. The other women hated her on sight, but she paid them no mind. She seemed delighted with the music, swaying her hips in time to the beating of the drums and laughing her way around the circle. It was as though she was moonlight personified, and Nalachi was pulled into her orbit."

Samantha sipped her wine, imagining what it would be like to step into a circle of dancers, laughing her way through a group of people she didn't know, beckoning to an unknown man from across the circle.

"The other men didn't stand a chance, did they?" Samantha asked.

"They did not – our Nalachi was in his prime and considered by many to be the prize catch in the village."

"And what was our fair maiden's name?" Samantha asked.

"Irmine, the lovely lady of moonlight and fire dancing, allowed Nalachi to dance with her through the evening, until the hours of the night drew to a close. Then, with the moon hanging low in the sky, she slipped away into the dark when he'd gone to bring them water."

"The classic sneak-out," Samantha murmured.

"Yes, but in this instance it was not lack of interest

in young Nalachi that pulled our lovely Irmine away. She had other reasons."

"Daylight?"

"Among other things. So Nalachi pursued her through the night to the cliffs, and found her at the water's edge. He asked her to stay with him – to be with him so he could know her better. She told him she must go. But to where? he wondered, and she replied that she had a boat around the way. Seeing that she refused to stay, Nalachi asked for something of hers – anything – so she would come back to him. Irmine, our tempting lady, pulled off the shell necklace that hung between her breasts and draped it over Nalachi's head. Needing to touch her as much as he needed his next breath, Nalachi grabbed her by the shoulders and pressed a passionate kiss to her mouth. When she pulled away, Irmine pressed her finger to his lips and told him to listen for her song, and he would know when she was coming back. She disappeared so quickly into the darkness of dawn that even Nalachi's trained eyes and ears couldn't see her boat or hear her in the water. He waited until at last, just from the horizon, he heard a voice so beautiful it brought tears instantly to his eyes."

"What did she sing?" Samantha asked, completely engrossed in the story.

"Where the starlight kisses the sea, this is where you'll find me. It won't be so long, for in your heart is my song," Lucas sang in a surprisingly sexy alto.

The air seemed to shimmer around them for a

moment as the notes trailed off, and a thick weight of tension pressed against Samantha's skin. A need, buried deep within her, cracked open and cried for attention. She understood longing and loneliness better than she would have liked.

"Heartsick, Nalachi returned to the water each night, necklace in hand, waiting to find his love where the starlight kissed the sea."

"But she never came again," Samantha breathed, commiserating with the sadness poor Nalachi must have felt.

"Ah, but the story isn't over. You see, she did return. Nalachi, mooning over the water one night, was shocked to see our pretty Irmine come dancing over the cliffs, radiating joy and light. It was in that moment his heart was truly lost – for she sang for him. Her heart had yearned for him as much as his for her. Under the blanket of stars that evening, they gave themselves to each other, worshiping each other's body and soul under the brilliant light of the full moon," Lucas said.

"Yeah, Irmine! Get yours, girl," Samantha laughed.

Lucas nodded in agreement. "Yes, Miss Irmine certainly had her fun with Nalachi. However, it turns out she was a love-him-and-leave-him type, for when he woke, huddled against the wall of the cave in the early morning light, she was gone again," Lucas said.

"Oh, Nalachi. It's hard learning you're a one-night stand." Samantha clucked her tongue.

"Happen to you before?" Lucas slid a glance to her.

"A time or two in college. It's never a good feeling," Samantha said, fudging a bit. She'd never been one for one-night stands or fooling around outside of a relationship, but she didn't want to appear dreadfully prudish to this man.

"I agree. It certainly isn't a good feeling," Lucas said, his eyes seeming to see more in the light from the twinkle lights strung between the trees. "However, Nalachi didn't have to know that feeling for long. In just a matter of weeks, she was back once more for another fabulous night."

"Let me guess – on the full moon?"

"Correct," Lucas said, draining the last of the wine bottle into their glasses. "And after a few months of this, our Nalachi figured it out as well. During her absences, he suffered terribly – so lovesick with missing Irmine that he began to lose weight. He began taking his boat out for hours at a time, and though he provided plenty of fish for his village due to the hours he spent on the water, his mother worried for him. She told him, one night, that he must bring the girl home. Make her stay at all costs. You see, his mother couldn't bear to lose her son. The next time Nalachi was with Irmine, his mother's words stayed in his head, and he bound her to him after their lovemaking. Despite her protests and her begging, he kept her. And as the light of day began to dawn, he received the biggest shock of his young life."

"She was a mermaid?"

"That she was. On land, as the sun began to rise,

Irmine began to gasp for breath, begging to be put in the water. When Nalachi realized that he was killing her, he ran to the water, carrying her, and dove in. As he unwound the cords that bound them, she turned in front of him."

"From woman to mermaid?"

"She did, finally showing her secret to him. She tried to get away, but he held her, floating in the water, as the shock and awe of it washed over him. 'You can't know of me – of us,' Irmine told Nalachi. He promised to tell not a soul. Told her he loved her for just what she was. Begged to go with her. 'I must go now or I will die,' Irmine insisted. And so he let her go, for even our dreamer Nalachi understood that love will never tie you down – it will only set you free."

"Oh, this is so sad. Did he ever see her again?"

"He did, but only once more. As trade picked up between the villages, Nalachi was summoned to work with one of the most important trade vessels on the island, and soon he was traveling between islands frequently and was away for every full moon for the next six months. It's said Irmine visited their spot on the beach, and her heart was broken – Nalachi did not love her as he had said; she knew he must be disgusted by her mermaid form."

"Oh!" Samantha let out a little gasp of sadness.

"Indeed. Irmine also carried another secret – one she had wanted to share with great joy with Nalachi, but she couldn't find him to tell him."

"She was pregnant," Samantha guessed, and Lucas tapped his glass to hers in a cheers.

"She was. Pregnant with twins. Now, in the mermaid world, it's said, babies are always a blessing and celebrated with great joy and reverence. But Irmine's father, having discovered she was pregnant by a human, was furious and forbade her to return to the island's shores. He feared humans, as he'd seen how much destruction they were capable of. He kept Irmine away from the island, hoping to protect her during her delicate time so that she could have healthy babies. However, in forbidding her to go, he inadvertently brought this tragic love story to an end," Lucas said, sighing a little.

"I don't know if I can hear this. I so want them to have a happy ending!" Samantha cried.

"I know, it's a bit heartbreaking – sort of a star-crossed lovers kind of thing. You see, Irmine never came to look for Nalachi when it wasn't a full moon, so she didn't see him walking the shoreline looking for her when he did return to the island. Finally, after many months, he returned home from a voyage on the night of a full moon. Barely stopping to hug his mother and present her with all the goods from his travels, Nalachi returned to the shore and his favorite little fishing boat. Ignoring the clouds on the horizon, which any sailor would know meant heavy storms were coming, Nalachi rowed himself out, his eyes searching the water, praying that he would find the one woman whose song he still carried in his heart."

"Oh, no," Samantha said.

"He was so focused on studying the waves that he didn't pay attention to the tell-tale signs of a reef. His hull scraped against it, cracking in two, and soon he was taking on water. Desperately, Nalachi looked back for land, trying to judge whether he could swim the distance. At the same time, the storm hit in all its ferocity. Nalachi clung to a bit of his boat with all his strength – and in his last moments, he began to sing the song she'd given to him," Lucas said.

Samantha was surprised to find tears pricking her eyes. "Did she come? Please tell me she came," Samantha whispered.

"She did, with her two daughters at her side. She found him as the life left him. He was too far gone for her magick to save him, you see? But he knew she was there, and he smiled at her as she cradled him in her arms, his head on her breast, his daughter's faces peering over his arm. And when his soul left his body, she kept it – forged into the shape of a pearl which she strung on a necklace. It's said she still sings each night to warn the sailors away from the treacherous reefs, and for those who do perish there, she turns their souls into pearls of the sea – singing even louder so that their lovers across the water will know she's caring for them in the afterlife."

"Oh… that's beautiful and horribly tragic at the same time," Samantha said, wiping a tear from her eye.

"But at last Irmine knew that she really was loved.

And now, as mother of the sea, she sings her songs of love and protection from the shore of the cliffs."

"And so they named this island after her," Samantha said. "I… I really appreciate the whimsy and beauty of that. So many places just get named for the first man to plant his stick in the ground and say 'This is my land.' The fact that the name has held through all these years…well, even if it is just a myth, I think it's wonderful."

"Who says it's just a myth?" Lucas asked, a wry smile on his face.

"Do you believe in mermaids?" Samantha turned to look at him, tilting her head so that the flower crown slipped a bit and she had to push it back up.

"Of course," Lucas said easily.

"You do? I'm shocked," Samantha laughed. "Why?"

"It's so much more boring not to believe, don't you think? I always like to believe that there's something magickal just waiting for us over the horizon."

Irma pulled away from where she'd leaned her head against the windowsill of the kitchen, the perfect spot for Samantha's and Lucas's voices to carry to her on the breeze. Brushing a tear from her eye, she pushed her shoulders back and turned to do the washing up.

"You still miss him, don't you?" Mirra asked, coming to wind her arms around her mother.

"I always will," Irma admitted.

"He's with us. You can see his soul swimming with us on the full moon," Jolie said, hugging her mother from the other side.

"I'll never stop loving that man. I hope one day you'll both know that sort of love." Irma patted them both and then pulled away. "That's enough melancholy for now. I have cookies to bake."

CHAPTER 15

"You don't have to walk me to my door," Samantha said, her nerves kicking up as Lucas left the garden with her. Walking her to the door meant she'd be presented with the decision of inviting Lucas in, and she wasn't sure if she was capable yet of doing something so frivolous as having a romp with a man she'd just met yesterday.

"I am a gentleman," Lucas demurred and Samantha shut her mouth, not wanting to sound ungrateful or rude. They silently climbed the stairs of the quiet villa until they stood in front of her weathered door.

"Um, this is me," Samantha said, gesturing to the door.

"Good, then my job is done." Lucas smiled down at her and Samantha felt heat flash through her body. He towered over her, all tanned muscles and warm green eyes, and she wanted to shock him by grabbing his hand and pulling him into the room.

"Thank you for sharing the wine with me, and for telling me that lovely story about the island," Samantha said.

"Since you paid for dinner tonight," Lucas said, leaning casually against the wall, neatly caging her in so that her back bumped against the door, "I owe you. Can I take you out tomorrow?"

"I… well, you don't owe me anything. It was just a bit of cheese and some wine, it's not really a big deal…"

Lucas silenced her with a kiss, shocking her by brushing his lips lightly across hers while she was still speaking, causing her words to trail off as her hands came up to his shoulders. The man took his time, easing her slowly against the door, letting his lips slide gently over hers, until the breath all but left her body and she moaned lightly into his mouth.

"Is that a 'yes, Lucas, I'd love to go out with you tomorrow' moan?" he teased, and Samantha blushed, her insides a knot of lust and aching and embarrassment.

"Yes, um, that would be nice," Samantha said, biting her lip.

Lucas raised a finger and traced her lips before bending over once more to kiss her – the most featherlight of kisses – before pulling away.

"Until tomorrow then. Sweet dreams," he said, strolling down the stairs and out the front door while Samantha tried not to melt into a puddle on the floor.

He'd kissed her.

And asked her out tomorrow.

Oh my god. She had a date tomorrow. And she'd had one tonight. And the man was *hot*.

Samantha squealed and ran inside, pouncing on her cell phone.

"Lola, you'll never believe this."

Deciding another glass of wine was called for while she stayed up to chat with Lola, Samantha opened a bottle, poured a glass, and relaxed on the bed.

"I love the name. Is he a good kisser?" Lola asked.

"He is, at least from what I can tell." Samantha found herself giggling into the phone like a schoolgirl.

"You kissed him already! I love this slutty side of you," Lola said.

"That was not slutty," Samantha protested.

"Well, for you it was. For me I would've shagged the man six ways to Sunday by now, but we're different."

Samantha felt heat course through her body at the thought of 'shagging' Lucas, as Lola had so delicately put it.

"I… I need a little time here. But I'm trying my best to channel my inner Lola."

"Good. I love what I'm hearing. Wear one of your new dresses tomorrow and do something foolish," Lola ordered.

"I will. Or at least I'll try," Samantha said.

"Have you managed to ignore your family?" Lola asked.

"Yes, I messaged them to let them know I was on holiday. The response was… well, it was pretty awful."

"Let me guess – you're foolish, get back to work, you'll never get anywhere in this company if you run away from your responsibilities, no daughter of mine shirks her work." Lola deepened her voice to mimic Sam's dad.

"Pretty much. With an added touch of how embarrassed they'll be at the country club with all the talk about me not getting the promotion and skipping town."

"For fuck's sake. You didn't skip the country. You're not on the lam. You took a holiday for the first time in years after clawing your way up the corporate ladder. I can't deal with them, I swear to god. You need to listen to me,"

Lola all but barked, "and hear every word. You have done nothing wrong. You not only deserve this vacation, but you have my permission to do every last thing you want that you know they'd hate. *Comprende*?"

"I know. I know. I know. You're completely right. I know I haven't done anything wrong. It doesn't stop it from hurting, is all," Sam said.

"When are you going to stop seeing yourself through their eyes?" Lola asked. "Because I think you're amazing exactly as you are. Well, especially this new and improved vacation-version of you. I suspect you like this version of you too."

Sam laughed. "You know what? I kind of do."

"Then own it, girl."

CHAPTER 16

When the phone began ringing the next morning, Samantha gave in to the inevitable. She'd spent another decadent night lying naked beneath the crisp white sheets – and wasn't that sad, that the most decadent thing she'd done in years was to sleep without a nightie? With a sigh and a yearning glance at the coffee pot across the room, Samantha answered her phone.

"Good morning, Mother," Samantha said, looking at the clock and noticing it was around breakfast time back home. Her mother would be preparing a light breakfast for her father, as she always did, while he watched the news and complained about the state of politics.

"I shouldn't have to call you this many times for you to answer," her mother's crisp voice answered. "One moment, your father would like to speak with you."

"That's really great," Samantha said, a little too

loudly. "I'm glad to hear you're doing well." But she was talking to air as her mother passed the phone across their granite counter to her father.

"Samantha." Her father's brisk tone, one that had made many a junior partner cower, sliced through the phone at her.

"Father," Samantha said, pinching a pleat in the bedsheet.

"That's enough of this Caribbean nonsense. You'll come home and make apologies to Paradiso for skipping town," her father ordered. "If you're lucky they'll take you back, though it's not likely you'll have another shot at the CFO position after this irrational behavior. It's best that word doesn't get out that you're unreliable. We'll expect you home this evening."

"They can't fire me for taking a vacation," Sam protested.

"They can if you take it at the last minute without giving notice," her father shot back.

"Then that's their choice. I'm sure I can find a company that won't make me defer my vacations for years," Samantha said, feeling the old pain lace her stomach as she tried, once again, to make her father hear her.

"You've already shown that you haven't worked hard enough, or you would have gotten the promotion. Do you really think it's wise to add to that image by taking off at a moment's notice for a jaunt through the Caribbean? Haven't I taught you that every action has a consequence? Just what do you think will happen as a result of this careless behavior of yours? If I were your boss, you'd be fired." Her father was in full-on rant mode. "That's what's wrong with young people these days. They think they can jump around from job to job, never putting in the tough work. They're always talking about wanderlust and living their lives. On what salary, may I ask? How are they going to live if they can't put food in their mouths? It's like nobody cares about putting in a hard day's work anymore. Instead they're flitting around taking Instagram photos on the latest popular beach locale and talking about making money from blogging. Blogging – what a joke. Like anybody wants to read what they have to say. You know what people want?"

Samantha opened her mouth to reply, but she knew it was useless.

"People want someone they can rely on. A lawyer or a doctor, to be exact. And when they pay people to handle their accounts, they expect that person to be there."

"They also can expect, and reasonably so, that the person they are paying to do said job is also human and has a life," Samantha sighed and pinched her nose where a dull ache had settled.

"What life? You don't have a husband or kids. Not even a dog to let out. Your life is your work. The day after you lose a huge promotion is exactly the day you need to step it up – coming in early and showing your willingness to do anything to work harder. Yet you're willing to chance the one thing that makes up your life? Your job? I don't get people like you." Her father's words jabbed at her, as they always did, and Samantha felt her shoulders slumping. She wanted to curl up in bed and hide, like she was a little girl again, weeping into the pillows after being grounded for whatever infraction she'd incurred this time.

"I haven't done anything wrong," Samantha said. "You seem unable to grasp that fact. I have done nothing legally, morally, or ethically wrong by taking my first vacation in years – vacation time that I am entitled to by my contract with my company."

"Bah, that's bullshit. You're constantly on vacation. They fly you everywhere and treat you to beautiful suites in the best hotels around the world. Don't act like you haven't gotten a vacation. People like you who whine about their jobs don't ever understand that the grass isn't always greener on the other side. Do you know what the workforce is like these days? There's a million people who would die for your job. If you're not careful, you'll be out on your butt quicker than you can say unemployment line. Now, be a good girl and get on that plane and go apologize to your new boss."

Samantha closed her eyes and forced herself to take a deep breath. Then another. She'd been on the receiving end of one variation of this tirade or another for most of her life. It didn't matter what she said or did, her parents insisted they knew best. It was their way or the highway, and if she didn't follow what they wanted then she was being difficult. God, she hated being labeled the bad one. How was she 'difficult' for choosing an occupation outside of law? It wasn't even that far outside of it, but she still had to hear grief about it years later. And the problem was? She usually did fall in line. Most of Sam's life had been tiny rebellions against her parents, just enough to try and get them to allow her to be herself instead of who they thought she should be. Just once, she wanted them to see her for who she was – an adult who could make her own choices.

So sure was her father that Samantha would do what he'd ordered that he was already handing the phone back to her mother. But not before he heard what she said next.

"I don't remember asking your opinion." Samantha clenched the phone and blinked back the tears that spiked her eyes, listening to the silence that greeted her as her stomach flipped into a complicated series of knots. She imagined it was like the moment when someone pulled the pin on a grenade.

"Oh, you think you know it all? You want to be like your friend Lola, who flits from job to job and man to man with no care for her future or her responsibilities? You're already probably too old to have children, and no man is going to want to marry someone who can't even hold down a job. You'd be wise to listen to my opinion before you ruin your life. But what do I know? I'm just the most successful attorney in this city and a man who has raised an extremely – well, *mostly* successful family. Which is more than you can say for yourself. Do what you want, Samantha, go be a feminist or whatever it is you're doing now and act like I've done nothing for you. I've only paid your way through college and opened every door possible for you. But of course, you'd know better. Have a nice life."

Tears poured down Sam's cheeks and all she could do was shake her head silently into the phone, willing her father to not be so harsh on her. There were so many things wrong with this conversation that she could barely wrap her head around them all. What was wrong with being a feminist? She was female, after all. And as far as she was concerned, being a feminist just meant she wanted the same opportunities as a man would have. If one of her brothers had taken off on a last-minute vacation, her family would have wished him well and told him to send pictures. How was this remotely fair?

"Now, Samantha, you know you shouldn't antagonize your father." Her mother's cool voice slipped through the phone and Sam closed her eyes, wishing that her mother would – just once – side with her and not the men of their family. But irrespective of her mother's fierceness as an attorney, she somehow still managed to cater to the men in her family while holding her own daughter to an entirely different standard.

"I'd say he's the one being antagonizing," Samantha said, not caring if she sounded bitchy.

"You know how he gets after he watches the news. He needs someone to vent it on."

"I'm not one of his employees. I'm his daughter. He just told me to have a nice life. As in, he's cutting me out of his life because I won't follow his directives."

"You need to think about what he says. He gets passionate about things. But it's only because he wants you to be your best."

"What about wanting what is best for me? *Me*. Not what he thinks is best. Not what you think is best. Why can't you both trust me to decide what is best for me? Even if you don't understand it? Even if it's not what you want?" Samantha cried.

"Now, Samantha. Of course we want what's best for you. But your father is right – your job is important. You don't have anything else in your life. It wouldn't be smart to be careless with it."

"Nice evasion, Counselor," Samantha said, bitterness lacing her voice.

"You'll do what you want anyway. You always do." Her mother's voice took on a surprisingly resentful tone that made Sam's back go up.

"What I… oh please. If I had done what I wanted, I would have never gone into accounting. Instead I'd have gone out west for college, pursued a teaching degree like I wanted, and would have met or married someone like Noah. Instead I'm stuck in a corporate job, coming to your house every Sunday to hear about how well everyone else in the family is doing with their promotions and kids while you all make pointed barbs about me still being single. Please, tell me, how I am doing anything I actually want in my life?"

"Nobody's forcing you to come to Sunday dinner, Samantha. Though it's not like you have a lot of other plans anyway."

"Goodbye, Mother. Don't plan for me to be at Sunday dinner anytime soon. When you're ready to accept me for me, I'll be here. Just like I've always been. Waiting for you to stop trying to force me into being something I'm not."

"Oh Samantha, you were always prone to dramatics. I really don't have time for this right now; I have a nine o'clock meeting."

"Standing up for myself is not being dramatic…"

Samantha's voice trailed off as her iPhone showed that the call had already been disconnected.

There it was – another conversation where her parents spewed at her, but refused to listen to what she had to say. It was what made them excellent lawyers – this singlemindedness in getting their point across – but did they need to use those tactics on her?

And at what cost?

Lola had been absolutely right to tell Sam to ignore her parents. If only she'd listened.

CHAPTER 17

A light tapping at her door drew her head up from where she'd buried her face in the pillows after the phone call with her parents. Sometimes she wondered if she was too sensitive for her family. She wished she didn't care so much what they thought of her – was there a class she could take to learn how to toughen up? Perhaps she just needed good old-fashioned therapy, she thought, as she tugged a cover-up over her head and padded lightly to the door.

"Oh, Sam, you *are* in here. I was just going to drop off some fresh beach towels and some mango I…" Irma trailed off as she took in Samantha's face. "My goodness, what's wrong?"

"Do I look that bad?" Samantha grumbled, though she was well aware how she looked after a crying jag.

"Let's just say it doesn't take much to guess you've

been crying. Is there anything I can do?" Irma asked, her hands full of towels and eyes full of concern.

"Oh, no, thank you," Samantha said, slightly embarrassed. This woman must think she was nuts. It was hard admitting to someone as self-assured and confident as Irma that she felt like the tightly wound string holding her life together was quickly unraveling. "It's nothing. I'll be just fine."

Irma walked to a small table and put the towels and plate of fruit down, turning with her hands on her hips. Immediately, Samantha wanted to hunch her shoulders. She felt like she was about to get her third scolding of the day.

"Who did this to you?" Irma demanded and Samantha's mouth dropped open.

"Who?"

"Yes, who made you cry? Is it Lucas? I'll go down and let him have a piece of my mind if that's the case," Irma said, her blue eyes bright, like she was a mama bear protecting her young.

"Oh, no, please don't. It's not him – he was lovely. Really," Samantha protested.

"I know I'm crossing a serious line here when it comes to guests and their privacy, but it makes me so upset to see someone as young and lovely as you so… burdened. What can I do to help?" Irma asked, crossing her arms over her chest. Today she wore flowing purple, and her hair was woven into a braided crown. She couldn't have looked more like a queen if she'd tried, Sam thought.

"Nothing, really. It's kind of you to care. I just need to let go of some stuff, I guess." Samantha shrugged a shoulder.

"What are your plans for the day?" Irma asked, changing the subject, which gave Sam a chance to breathe. She was worried that if she talked about how much her parents hurt her – and continued to hurt her – she might cry for days. And what kind of vacation would that be?

"I haven't even gotten that far, to be honest. It's been a rough morning," Samantha said.

"Why don't you have a nice little breakfast on your balcony and meet me in the garden in a bit? Put on your suit. I'll show you a pretty spot for an adventure," Irma said, passing by without touching her or offering a hug. She seemed to sense that Sam would have balked at the gesture. The last thing Sam needed to do was sit in her room and sulk all day on this beautiful island, so she turned and mustered a smile for Irma.

"That would be great. Thank you. And thanks for bringing the towels and the fruit. I'll be down in a bit."

"Put on your new suit. It's time for a new Sam."

What was with these women at the Laughing Mermaid, Sam wondered as she unwrapped the mango slices and sipped a cup of coffee on her balcony. Curling her feet under her, she watched as one of the parrots from yesterday flew to a tree nearby and cocked its head at her.

"You think you're getting a piece of my mango?" Sam asked, raising an eyebrow at it.

The parrot squawked, hopping from limb to limb until it teetered delicately on the side of her balcony, its eyes intent on her plate of mango.

"I don't care how pretty you are," Samantha lectured. "If you swoop down here and take my breakfast without asking, you'll be dinner."

The bird squawked again, this time fluffing out its wings as if to tell her to chill out.

"And here I am taking my anger out on a poor parrot," Samantha sighed. Untucking her legs, she cut a sliver of mango for the bird and leaned over to place it on the edge of the balcony. Sitting back, she waited.

The parrot eyed her coolly.

"Oh, all right then. I'm sorry. I didn't mean to say I'd cook you for dinner. You can have some mango," Sam said. That was it, she'd definitely gone over the edge into crazytown if she was having full-on conversations with a bird.

The parrot hopped its way down the balcony and delicately took the mango before flying back to the safety of a tree branch. Oddly pleased at its reaction, she cut off a few more scraps and left them on the balcony ledge before going inside to dig through her bag of new clothes.

Maybe Irma was right – could it be as simple as that?

New suit, new Sam.

It was worth a try.

CHAPTER 18

It was just a bikini, Sam told herself. Standing in front of the mirror in the bathroom, she scanned her reflection. Charlene had been right – red was a good color for her. Granted, it would look a bit better if she'd gotten herself a spray tan, but there wasn't much she could do about that now. Maybe later today she'd read her novel and catch a little sun to add some glow to her skin.

Otherwise, Sam thought it best not to look too long in the mirror. She certainly couldn't claim the curves of Jolie or Mirra, but she looked fine in the bikini, she decided. Just fine. Before she could talk herself out of wearing it, she wrapped the matching red sarong around her body and grabbed her beach tote, sailing from the bedroom and down to the garden.

The little side path that led to the palm garden and out to the beach was dappled with artwork and twinkle lights, and today Sam took the time to stop and examine as she went. Behind one palm tree a metal shark statue lurked; from another, bright blue glass fisherman balls hung in nets, and pretty orchids poked out from some brush. Lace-looking lanterns hung from a plumeria tree, and twinkle lights were strung about in no particular order. It should have been messy, but for some reason the total effect was charming and cozy.

Sam wished she could decorate like this – with a touch of whimsy. Instead her downtown condo was done up in cool grey tones, all soothing and precise and gently pretty, but not a touch of whimsy to be found. Sam resolved to find some cool art while she was here and have it shipped back for the big empty wall over her low-slung leather couch.

She stopped suddenly when she saw Lucas talking to Irma down by the water. Shit, shit, shit, she scolded herself, couldn't she have wrapped her sarong higher on her body? They both turned her way before she had a chance to do so, and it would look weird to stand there and stare at them while fumbling with her sarong, so Sam soldiered on. Don't be such a nervous geek, Sam lectured herself, and plastered a smile on her face as she approached. You've been kissed before. You've had sex. For god's sake, you've even been engaged. Act like a grown woman.

"Good morning," Lucas said, his teeth flashing white in his tanned face.

Sam promptly tripped over her feet in the sand, and Irma caught her arm to steady her.

"Flip-flops in the sand – never a great idea," Irma said, smoothly covering Sam's embarrassment by nodding down to her sandals. "Most of us go barefoot around here as much as we can."

"Good idea," Sam said, bending to slide her shoes off and toss them by a chair.

"Lucas here was kind enough to lend us his kayak. I thought we'd go for a paddle and explore," Irma said brightly.

Sam gulped, looking out at the wide expanse of ocean in front of them. "Out there?"

"Unless you planned to kayak in the pool?" Lucas laughed at her and Sam realized she was being ridiculous.

"Of course out there." Sam waved at the water. "It's just so… big."

"We'll stay close to the shoreline," Irma smiled. "I promise to get you home safe."

"Um, sure. What should I bring? What do I need?" Sam asked, looking down into her tote.

"Put your hat on." Irma gestured to the rolled straw hat that stuck out of her bag. "Sunscreen and that's it. Leave everything else here."

"Will it be safe?" Sam asked, worried about her wallet and iPhone in her bag.

"Perfectly. The girls are home," Irma smiled.

"Or I can watch it for you," Lucas said. "That way

you'll have to come see me after your paddle."

"I mean… whatever works," Sam said, feeling a little breathless as she lost herself looking at his chest.

"That's right kind of you, Lucas. Why don't you carry that for her," Irma immediately decided, and set off down the beach.

Lucas grabbed the straps of her tote, gently tugging until she let them go, and slung it over his shoulder. An involuntary giggle slipped from her at the sight of the bright pink pom-pom bag on his shoulder.

"What? Is pink not my color?" Lucas asked.

"It looks great on you," Sam laughed.

"As does that suit. Red sure is your color, Sam," Lucas said, his gaze lingering on her bikini. Sam felt her whole body flush and she tripped again in the sand. Mortified, she looked out over the water, surprised to find another sheen of tears hitting her eyes. Why did everything have to be so tricky for her?

"Bring that sultry thing you do down a notch or two, Lucas. Can't you see Sam needs to take it slow?" Irma demanded, and Sam decided that her humiliation was officially complete.

"It's fine. Really," she stammered.

"I have taken it slow. Didn't I leave her at her doorway last night with a chaste kiss? That was very gentlemanly of me," Lucas countered.

Sam opened her mouth, but Irma overrode her.

"A woman like Sam needs to be swept off her feet.

You can't just leer at her and make her blush," Irma said.

Okay, *now* her mortification was complete.

"But I like how pretty she looks when her cheeks flush pink," Lucas argued right back.

Did she look pretty when she blushed? No one had ever told her that before.

"There's plenty of time to make her blush," Irma said as they arrived at his dock.

"And trust me, I am more than excited to take that time and do so," Lucas said.

Sam's face and body flamed in response.

"See?" Lucas said, and surprised Sam by bending over to brush his lips over her cheek. "Beautiful."

"Um, thank you. I'm not, I don't need…" Sam took a breath. "Okay, forget it. I'm a mess right now. Irma is right. I may need time. But usually I'm really a capable adult who can walk on her own two feet and form sentences and lead boardrooms full of high-level executives. I have no idea where that person is at the moment, but I promise you, most of the time I have my shit together."

"See? She's a ballbreaker. She doesn't need you to defend her," Lucas laughed at Irma, reaching over to tug on her braid.

"Everyone needs someone in their corner," Irma said, then turned toward the kayak tied to the dock. "Ready, Sam?"

Sam eyed the kayak balefully. A two-seater, it was

shiny yellow and rocked gently in the turquoise blue water. She briefly wondered how a death trap could look so innocuous and then shrugged. "I suppose so."

"Ever been in one of these before?"

"On a lake once, ages ago."

"Keep your balance in the center. Lucas, help her in," Irma said. She'd already tossed her purple caftan onto the dock and Samantha was shocked to see her rocking a decidedly tiny purple bikini, along with several stunning tattoos that entwined themselves around her legs, up her sides, and across her back – mermaids and fish and flowers galore.

"Wow. I was not expecting you to have tattoos, for some reason. They're beautiful," Sam said, following her waist-deep into the water.

"Always keep people guessing, Sam," Irma smiled at her across the water – such an open and genuine smile that Sam found herself grinning right back.

"Can I be you when I grow up?"

Irma tossed her hair over her shoulder and laughed. "I'll let you know."

CHAPTER 19

Lucas watched them go. In her slip of a bikini, Irma deftly steered the kayak out, her braids tumbling down her back. Samantha sat up front, timidly dipping her paddle in the water, the large sunhat and slash of her red bikini painting a pretty picture.

He couldn't seem to stop himself from flirting with Sam. She dimpled up and blushed so delightfully every time he nudged the line of flirtation with her. He grinned as he thought about her stammering at the door last night and how he'd shocked her with a kiss. Lucas hadn't planned to move so fast with her – it was clear as glass that this woman needed time – but she'd been so flushed and awkward that he hadn't been able to help himself.

Lucas walked to the deck of his villa and deposited Sam's tote bag on one of his black-and-white striped lounge chairs. The bag was funky and bright, nothing at all like the woman Samantha presented herself as. He wondered what else he would reveal when he unwrapped the package.

It had been a long time since a woman had piqued Lucas's interest like Sam did. Perhaps it was because he recognized so much of himself in her. The lips that tightened too quickly, the hunched shoulders and tense demeanor – he'd been exactly the same when he was overworked in a job that had ultimately made him unhappy. It had made him a lot of money as well, as being a hedge fund manager can if one was good at it, but after a while he just wasn't up for the lifestyle.

The guys at the office thought he was insane. They'd had the best of it all – entrance to all the hottest clubs, VIP seating at the restaurants, beautiful women lining up to be with them. In theory, he'd won the game. He'd been on top of it all.

There'd been no reason for him to visit Siren Island when he first had. At the time, it was just one of those things you did when you had too much money – book a trip to an exotic locale with a group of friends and beautiful women. They'd chartered a plane, and as soon as it landed on the tiny island most of the group had started complaining about how hot it was and when were the cars arriving to take them to their rented villa.

But not Lucas. He'd been on a window seat at the back, headphones on and looking out the window when they'd landed. The plane had veered sharply over the cliffs at the end of the island where he could just make out a statue of a mermaid jutting out of the rocks. It had made him smile – the first real smile he'd had in ages, for something so simple as a pretty stone statue of a mermaid on tiny Siren Island. He might have lost his heart to the island in that moment.

That week had been fun, but this time Lucas had abstained from most of the partying and spent his time exploring the island solo. He rented a Jeep and went to the cliffs on one end of the island, and took a snorkel tour with a local guide on the other end. After one look at the colorful world that greeted him beneath the water, Lucas had vowed to become scuba-certified. That time in the water – the first time in years that nobody could talk to him or had needed anything from him – had been the most peaceful and meditative time he could remember. When they left the island, he had been determined to come back.

In a weird way, it had become a bit of an obsession of his. Sure, many people talked about retiring and moving to an island one day. But he actually did it, and far earlier than retirement age. It had been the loss of one of his partners – a good friend – that had done him in.

He couldn't say he'd been expecting the call, but it hadn't been all that much of a surprise either. Lucas still remembered it – crystal clear. He'd been standing at his office window, watching a spring storm roll over Lake Michigan when the phone had rung.

"It's Jack," another partner, Richard had said, his voice scarily toneless.

"What happened?" Lucas had pinched his nose, and hated the memory of what he'd said next. "We don't have to bail him out of jail again, do we? I'm getting sick of calling in favors to our lawyers."

"He's dead, Lucas. Overdosed at the party last night."

Lucas had dropped the phone, watching as lightning lit up the sky, and all he could think about in that moment was running away – away from it all. The pressures of the job, the pressures of keeping up appearances, the hard-partying lifestyles of the young and wealthy he hung out with. If he'd ever had an angel on his shoulder, it was the one that kept him from ever being interested in putting a drug up his nose.

And so he'd buried his friend, quit his job, and moved to an island. Alone.

Sure, he was lonely at times – though he often found more comfort in solitude than he did in being around people. Maybe he had some post-traumatic something going on from the intense social life he'd used to live. He'd had a fling with a woman or two who had passed through the island on holiday – he was human, after all. One of his more adamant ex-girlfriends had even made her way down and tried to convince him they belonged together. But he'd found that this life suited him, and she had quickly realized that without a Nordstrom and a Starbucks nearby, she just wasn't interested.

It had taken him a year or two before he'd finally relaxed and gotten into the island rhythm. He'd learned that things got done in their own time on the island, and that was that. It always worked out eventually. When Lucas had first discovered this villa was for sale, he almost didn't come by to take a look. It was a little further from town than he'd thought he wanted at the time. But, thank goodness, his realtor had pushed him into taking a look. Not only had he discovered his own little paradise, but it had come equipped with the most unique set of neighbors he'd ever had the privilege to know. He'd made many a new friend through the years living near their bed and breakfast, and he always enjoyed helping out the ladies of the Laughing Mermaid when they needed it.

Sam wasn't the first woman they'd nudged Lucas toward – or perhaps had nudged toward Lucas. But this one seemed different. Either because of the way she intrigued him or the way Irma was looking out for her. Protective. In almost a motherly way. Irma did love her wounded birds, Lucas thought.

Lucas wanted to peel back her layers and figure out what made her tick. Samantha was a ball of emotions – one moment she was fiercely learning to drive a stick shift and tearing off into town on a whim, and the next she was blinking back tears after a fairytale mermaid story. She was like a young colt, learning to walk for the first time. Jerky, skittish, and still excited about seeing the world.

He wondered if he would eventually get to see the real Samantha Jameson. If she trusted herself enough to just be.

Lucas hoped she'd show herself to him. Because he was fairly certain he was already well and thoroughly hooked.

CHAPTER 20

"It seems pretty calm," Sam said, relaxing marginally as they paddled slowly along the coastline, with no particular agenda in mind. This was nice, she realized. No tour company to tell her when to be back and nothing for her to be back for. Imagine living a life with this much freedom.

"It's a perfect day for a paddle. The trade winds are low and there's relatively little current. We'll have a nice easy time of it," Irma said.

"I can't get over how clear the water is. You really can just look straight down and see fish swimming around."

"We'll head out toward the reef by the cliffs. It's tricky to get to with bigger boats, so it's hardly fished – you can see loads of sea life there," Irma said. She guided Sam on how to paddle and they turned the boat toward the cliffs at the curve of the bay.

Once they were in an easy rhythm, again in no particular rush, Sam let out a deep exhale. This was certainly better than sitting in her room sulking over another tough phone call with her parents. It wasn't like they were giving her a passing thought, aside from perhaps checking their emails to see what flight she was coming home on. Because, of course, they would assume she'd follow their directive.

Instead, she was on the prettiest stretch of water she'd ever seen, with a new friend who she suspected didn't take shit from anyone, and she had not a thing planned for the day other than going to look at some fish and flirting with a sexy man.

All in all, Sam thought she could get used to this.

"It seemed like you were relaxing a bit, but then I felt this wave of tension go through you," Irma commented from behind her. "Your shoulders went from relaxed to tense again. Want to talk about it?"

"I doubt talking about it will change much. It's hard to change a situation with two immovable objects," Sam said, glancing over her shoulder at where Irma paddled patiently behind her. Once again she was struck by the backdrop – brilliant blue water and palm trees dotting the beach in little poofs of green.

"Want to try anyway?" Irma asked, her tone as placid as the water that lapped gently against the yellow hull of the kayak. She stopped paddling and let them drift for a while to give Sam some time to think.

"I guess… it's just that everything's kind of come to

a head. And I'm stepping back, or I guess out of, my life to take stock and realize what isn't working for me," Sam said.

"And what would that be?"

"All of it. Or I should say, none of it. Nothing is working for me. Not my job, not my family, and not finding love. So what's the point of it all? Why am I burning the candle at both ends for something I don't want?"

"Tell me about your job," Irma said, steering them gently away from a few rocks that poked from the water.

"It's a job anyone would dream of. Travel the world, manage luxury villa and boutique hotel accounts, and so on."

"But it's not what you dream of," Irma stated.

"I... it's not that I don't like working with numbers. Because I do. I actually really do, I enjoy how everything lines up neatly and how when you add numbers together the outcome is the same. Unlike people, where no matter which equation you try, they never give you the answer you expect." Sam shrugged a shoulder, stretching her legs so that the sun caught them.

"Did you leave your job?" Irma asked.

"I didn't. I have been working for years to get the CFO position. I never said no to anyone, or any trip. Where everyone else had family or prior responsibilities, I didn't. I did everything they asked me and went above and beyond. And still… I didn't get the promotion I'd been working for. They even told me it was all but guaranteed to be mine. I went to Japan on a day's notice for them," Sam said, feeling her shoulders tense again and the ball in her gut tighten. "And they gave the CFO to the guy who charms everyone in the office and passes his work off to everyone else."

"I don't like your employers much," Irma commented, surprising a laugh out of Sam. "Well? I don't. What kind of employer would use someone like that and not reward them for their hard work? It's unconscionable. And it's how you lose good people. Loyalty should be rewarded. Are you a good accountant? I'm sorry if that sounds rude – but are you?"

"Yes," Sam said, though she blushed at being so blunt about her skills. "Yes, I really am. Whenever they audit the accounts, mine always come back perfect."

"See? So it sounds to me like you have a shitty employer. What's the big deal with you taking a vacation?"

"I left the day after the CFO announcement. With no real warning to anyone."

"Like how they gave you less than a day to prepare to go to Japan?"

"I… well, yes, exactly like that," Sam said.

"So if they can do that to you, why can't you do that to them? Do you take vacation often?"

"I haven't, no," Sam said, tucking a strand of hair

behind her ear as the unjustness of her situation boiled in her stomach.

"Ever? How long have you been there?"

"Over seven years," Sam said.

"And you've never taken a vacation? You have every right to take one. I'm sorry, but you have been too good to them. Is that what's worrying you? Your tears this morning? Are you concerned you'll lose your job?"

"No, it's not the job – though yes, partly that is a concern," Sam said.

"I think it sounds like you'd be better off without them. That's no way to live your life," Irma said. "I'm sorry. That sounds harsh. It's your life and you absolutely should choose what to do with it. If you love this job, which it sounds like you don't, but if you actually do, I suggest taking your vacation time for some perspective, then going back and negotiating new terms with them on how you want your position to look."

Sam marveled at the honest advice. For once in her life, someone – aside from Lola, that is – was advising her to trust her own judgment and do what she wanted. It was refreshing to be treated as an adult who knew her own mind, instead of a child who needed constant corralling to do what others considered best for her.

"You're absolutely right, Irma. If I decide to keep this job – and doesn't that feel awesome to say? If *I* decide, not anyone else, then yes, I will most certainly go back and negotiate my terms. Because you know what? I am damn good at what I do," Sam said, feeling a little trill of excitement race through her at claiming that bit of power.

"And who else would decide if you keep your job? Isn't that for you to say?" Irma asked, beginning to steer them toward the cliffs that jutted proudly from the sparkling Caribbean sea.

"My parents. My brothers. My extended family. Everyone my parents talk to. Pretty much everybody seems to have an opinion on how I should be living my life," Sam grumbled. "Maybe that's an exaggeration. But mainly my parents. They're…"

"Controlling?"

"I was going to say overbearing," Sam sighed, dipping her paddle in the water. "But controlling would be the more apt word."

"How do they try to control you?"

"Basically they want everyone in the family to fall in line with what they know. Practice law, get married, have kids, stay in the lane," Sam bit out.

"What's wrong with being an accountant? That's a fairly admirable career, no?"

"It is. But it isn't law. Just like the man I really fell in love with wasn't an attorney. Just like I failed at holding the engagement together with the man they did want me to marry. Just like all the things. It doesn't seem to matter what I do – they have an opinion on it. The reason I was crying this morning when you found me is that they called me up and ordered me to get on a plane today. They're convinced I'll lose my job. And that would take them to a new level of embarrassment, because they're already dealing with the shock of me not getting this promotion and oh, what will people say?" Sam didn't realize it but she had begun stabbing the water with the oar, paddling them faster toward the rocks as her anger kicked up. "Who the fuck cares what anyone says about my job? It's mine. Not my parents'. Not their friends'. Why do I always have to do what they want? They think they know what's best for me. But did anyone ever just ask me what I wanted? Nobody did. Not my perfect brothers. Not my father. And certainly not my mother, who seems to have no problem kowtowing to the men in the family, though she's a brilliant woman and can stand on her own two feet. Why is she bending over backward taking care of them and then coming down so hard on me? I'm so tired of being told I'm the difficult one when all I've wanted to do is live my life free of their judgement. Just once, just *once* I would love for my family to see me as me. Just me. And accept that for what it is. I'm not a bad person." Sam was shocked to realize she was openly weeping again.

"No, you're not a bad person." Irma reached forward to gently pat Sam's shoulder. "It sounds like you've got some work to do."

"I know. I need to apologize to them and make things right," Sam said, automatically defaulting to a refrain that she had played out so many times in the past.

"Absolutely not! They owe you an apology, though I doubt you'll ever get one," Irma said, shocking Sam once more with her instant support. "I mean you'll need to work on changing your expectations of them. You keep allowing them into your life and getting the same results."

"Which is the definition of insanity," Sam said.

"So either you put boundaries up as to what you tell them, or change your expectations of how they'll react."

"I just want them to love me," Sam said. "Not control me. Just love me."

"People try to control what they fear," Irma said, her voice sad.

"What? Why would they fear me?" Sam asked, turning as much as she could in the kayak and looking at Irma. "I'm the least fearsome person in the world."

"Because you are going against what they know – what their safe zone is. And you've barely even stepped outside their safe zone. Imagine what would happen if you really embraced who you are."

"They'd probably hate me," Sam sighed.

"Or really envy you," Irma said. "You might have a freedom they've never known – one they wouldn't even know what to do with."

"Me?" Sam all but squeaked. "But they have all the money and prestige – they can do whatever they want."

"Not when everyone's watching, they can't. They've

built themselves their own little prison there. And you're an escaped inmate," Irma laughed.

"Well, shit, I've never looked at it like that," Sam said, captivated by the idea. "Me. A rebel. Who would've thought?"

"Who would've thought indeed?"

CHAPTER 21

They stayed in the boat for another hour or two, not that Sam was even remotely keeping track of time. Between the discovery of a mermaid statue on the cliffs and her delight at the hundreds of fish that swam below the kayak, she found herself lost in the enjoyment of the day.

"Irma, I want to thank you for taking me out today," Sam said as they returned to Lucas's dock. "Honestly, this was so much better than me sitting in the room and pulling myself deeper into a funk. You've shown me such beauty and given me a lot to think about."

"Don't think too much, you're on vacation," Irma said, hopping nimbly from the kayak and wading them in toward shore.

"I'm not sure I know how to switch that off," Sam said, smiling down at Irma.

"I think you need to learn how to have fun again.

Let loose a bit. Not live by anyone's expectations other than the ones you've set for yourself. Discover the joy in just being… just feeling in the moment." Irma reached out and brushed her hand over Sam's arm. "Channel your inner mermaid."

"My inner mermaid," Sam laughed, delighted at the concept. "And what would my inner mermaid do about that?"

They both looked to where Lucas sauntered down the beach toward the dock, his shorts riding low on his hips, a smile on his face for them.

"My inner mermaid may be naughtier than yours, because I'd take that man inside for an afternoon delight," Irma smiled and Sam threw her head back and laughed.

"I doubt I can do that," Sam said, blushing a bit at the thought of rolling around on the bed all salty from the ocean water, her hot skin brushing against his.

"Maybe just a taste then," Irma smiled and then turned to Lucas.

"You ladies look like you've had fun. Can I interest you in a bite to eat? I've got the grill going, thinking you might be hungry when you got back."

"I have some business to take care of, but I'm sure Sam would love to." Irma grinned at Sam and hummed the refrain from 'Afternoon Delight.'

Sam flushed again and, in lieu of answering, tried to gracefully slide from her seat on the boat. Instead she found herself with a mouth full of seawater, and wanted to just let herself sink to the bottom.

"You all right? Kayaks can be tricky to get out of," Lucas said, fishing her out of the water and setting her on her feet. Sam brushed her soaking hair from her face and snatched up her hat before it floated away along with the rest of her dignity.

"Yup, I meant to do that. Cool off from a hot day and all," Sam said, sticking her chin in the air.

"Oh, in that case," Lucas said and dunked her under the water again.

Sam came up sputtering. "Hey!" She laughed, splashing him.

"I'll leave you two. See you later, Sam, stop by if you need anything," Irma said, already hightailing it down the beach with a wave.

"Looks like you're stuck with me," Lucas said, grabbing her hand and dragging her from the water so that she stood in the sand, sopping wet.

"Looks like it. Do you have a towel for a girl to use?"

"That I do," Lucas said, and swung an arm comfortably over her shoulders. Sam tensed for a moment and then relaxed into him as they walked up the sand to the path that led to his villa.

The house itself was set back from the water and sheltered by palm trees. Whitewashed walls, cheerful blue trim, and an open-air living room greeted her as they reached the top of the path, along with a large dog of indistinguishable breed, who all but vibrated with energy.

"You have a dog," Sam stated more than asked, having come to a full stop.

"Yes, though at times I'm hard-pressed to call him a dog. More of a cat some days." Lucas slid a glance back to where Sam had stopped on the path. "Are you scared of dogs?"

"What's his name?" Sam whispered.

"His name is Pipin," Lucas said, looking back and forth from Pipin – who was clearly dying to leap excitedly on them, only his training holding him in one spot – to Sam, who stood frozen, with her hands to her lips. "Are you sure you're okay with dogs?"

"I've always wanted a dog," Sam breathed and dropped to her knees. "Come here, Pipin!"

The dog looked to his master for guidance. When Lucas waved him on, he dove down the path, all but tossing Sam end over end as he leapt on her in sheer joy, bathing her face in one long sloppy lick of love.

"Oh, aren't you the sweetest lump of fuzzy roly-poly cuteness," Sam gushed, burying her face in Pipin's coat. He writhed around her in joy, seeming to agree with her statement. "You're just the most handsome boy ever, aren't you?"

Pipin dropped to his back and rolled over, begging for tummy scratches. Sam laughed and readily indulged him, and for the first time in his life, Lucas found himself jealous of a dog.

"He seems to think so," Lucas said, smiling down at Sam as she continued to baby-talk Pipin, who lapped it up as though he never got love from anyone. Ever.

"He's just a total doll," Sam said. Giving Pipin one last pat, she straightened to wipe the slobber from her face and laughed up at Lucas.

His breath caught at the sight of her, hair tumbling wild from the water, her face alight with joy, her bikini a slash of red against the Caribbean blue of the sea behind her. She looked like an entirely different woman than the one who'd first arrived, buttoned up and miserable, forcing herself to relax without an agenda on the beach.

He wanted her.

It surprised him, the ferocity of his need. Not just sexually; he wanted to know what made her brain tick, who had hurt her so deeply – for she was clearly wounded – and he wanted to be the one to patch her back together. Reminding himself once more to go slow with her, he tossed her a friendly smile.

"Yes, Pipin chose me more than I chose him. Or perhaps we chose each other. He showed up on my doorstep one day, conveniently when I was grilling, and I couldn't bring myself to turn him away."

"Wormed his way into your heart, did he?" Sam bent down to pet a delighted Pipin once more.

"He was a bag of bones when I met him, if you can believe that." Lucas shook his head at Pipin, "I couldn't bear to let him starve. So, I began leaving some food out for him, letting him come back when he wanted to. It didn't take him long to discover that I had a couch. After that, he moved himself in."

"I'm surprised he didn't bring his friends along," Sam laughed again.

"He played it smart – if he shared he might not be king of the castle. Now he owns me and that's that," Lucas said.

"It's hard to imagine him skin and bones," Sam said as she eyed a decidedly healthy-looking Pipin.

"Are you fat-shaming him?" Lucas dropped his mouth open in pretend shock. Even Pipin seemed to understand and turned to look at her over his shoulder.

"No," Sam gushed, dropping to her knees again to cuddle Pipin. "I would never. He's the perfect amount of roly-poly."

"Good. We don't fat-shame in this house, do we, Pipin? No judgment here," Lucas said.

"That's good to hear," Sam said, standing and pinching her stomach, making a lame joke about being uncomfortable with her body in the bikini.

"I love your body, Sam. You should never cover it up in a one-piece," Lucas said. When she looked at him in shock, he turned away with a smile to walk over to his grill. He'd have to ease her into accepting compliments, he realized.

"What is with everyone being so nice here? I swear, it's like the nicest island of people," Sam decided as she came to stand by the grill. "Are you all just drinking the happy juice or something?"

"Maybe we are – it's hard not to be easy-going in this paradise. Plus, there's nothing wrong with making people feel good about themselves, right?"

Sam leaned her hip against the table and studied Lucas as he deftly put chicken sate and rounds of pineapple onto the grill, which sizzled as the pineapple juices hit the flame.

"No, there's nothing wrong with that at all. You've a lovely home here, Lucas. I love how open-air concept it is – it kind of just embraces the ocean, doesn't it?" Sam said.

"Would you like a quick tour while the chicken cooks?"

"I'd love one," Sam admitted, and bent quickly to dry her feet – which Pipin took as another invitation to slather her face with his tongue. "Pipin! So many kisses."

"He gets a little overexcited," Lucas said.

"That's fine by me. It's nice to be wanted," Sam said absently as she wiped her face with the towel and followed Lucas into the open-air living room. Rendered cement floors flowed into other rooms; wide leather couches dominated one area, with hardwood tables and chairs tucked into another. Color was brought in with pops of blues and reds in the vibrant island photos that covered the walls.

"These photos are great," Sam said, nodding to a particularly charming one of a seahorse.

"Thanks. I have fun taking them," Lucas said as he led Sam down a hallway to the bedrooms.

"They're yours?" Sam gushed.

"Yes, just a hobby. I love diving, so it's fun to try and capture some images of what I see underwater."

"Isn't diving scary? What if a shark comes?"

Lucas turned and smiled at her.

"Then I jump in the water and take a picture of it."

"Oh. Hmmm," Sam said, unable to form sentences for a moment because they stood about two inches apart in the doorway of his bedroom. Her brain suddenly skewed to danger of another sort as she eyed the massive driftwood bed that dominated the room. It shocked her to realize that she wanted to drop her towel and tug Lucas into the room and indulge in all sorts of deliciously naughty things that she was too prudish to even come up with. But if she was a mermaid, Sam thought, she'd know what to do.

"Pretty bed," Sam managed, swallowing past the need.

"Thanks. I had it custom-made by a builder on the island. He also made similar ones for the guest rooms," Lucas said, continuing down the hallway and popping open doors as he went. The villa was lovely, arranged so that guests could have their privacy, and done up in cool soothing tones that invited one to relax after a hot day in the sun. Sam found herself wishing her life could be like that – spending more time outside and less time in conference rooms.

"Let's go check on lunch," Lucas said, reaching out for her hand and tugging her back down the hallway toward the patio. A little tendril of warmth trailed up her arm at his touch and she delighted in how good something as simple as holding hands made her feel. It felt nice to be wanted, she realized, just for her presence alone – not for her job or who her parents were.

"Your house is beautiful," Sam said as Lucas deftly plated the food and slid it onto a stone table already set with plates. Opening a small cooler, he brought out a pitcher of what looked to be tea. "Do you rent or own?"

"Thank you. I rented here for years, I'm not sure why – I could have saved myself money if I had just purchased a place early on. I guess I was waiting for the right place to find me. And when this one did, well… I wasn't even going to look at it as it was further from town than I thought I wanted. But, well, just look at this." Lucas gestured to the beach and the stunning ocean view that presented itself. "It's hard to say no to that view. Plus, I quickly realized I didn't mind being further out from town. I'm a bit of a homebody, I've learned."

"Were you not always?" Sam asked, sampling a bit of the grilled pineapple. The warm sweetness of the fruit exploded on her tongue and she almost groaned in ecstasy. Why had she never thought about grilling pineapple before?

"No. But it took me years to realize that the party-hard 'see and be seen' lifestyle was not something I wanted. The costs are too great," Lucas said, a shadow passing over his handsome face.

Sam studied him for a moment. "What was the cost for you?" she asked softly.

"I lost a friend to drugs," Lucas said, his tone flat as he took a slug of his iced tea. "It crushed me."

"Were you with him? Doing drugs with him?" Sam asked, realizing just how little she knew about the man who sat before her. Pipin came over and nudged her with his nose, looking hopefully up at her plate of chicken.

"No – well, not the drugs part. But I certainly participated in the fast lifestyle of clubs, drinking, and being seen at the best places in town. That 'money talks' sort of way of life. Jack, my friend and one of my partners, took that further by getting too deeply into cocaine. Turns out he had also had a weak heart. The mix ultimately ended him. Losing him… well, it brought my life into perspective."

"And so you ended up here," Sam surmised. "What did you do for work?"

"We were hedge fund managers," Lucas said, smiling a little at Sam's look of surprise. "I know, hardly the ones that you'd think would party hard. But there was just so much money floating around and we were young. I think it was too much altogether."

"What happened when you left the company?"

"The other partners weren't happy with me, but they could hardly give me a hard time for it. Losing Jack made me realize that I didn't want to spend the rest of my life working for other people and living a life that, ultimately, left me empty inside."

"And your family? Did they support your choice?"

"It's just my mom. My father took off when I was young. She worked several jobs to support me growing up. Part of why I worked so hard was to give back to her. But she's always wanted me to be happy, and I think she worried when I was at the firm. She seems much more content now. Granted, she loves having her island retreat to come to, so I don't think she's complaining," Lucas laughed.

"Where does she live?"

"I moved her out of Chicago and bought her a condo in Florida. She's got a great little group of friends down there and she's enjoying her life, even though I couldn't get her to fully retire. The woman does like to work. She's part-time at a garden center. Now her biggest gripe is her lack of grandchildren."

"Do you want kids?" Sam asked, tilting her head as she studied him. She wondered what kind of father he would be.

"No, I've never particularly wanted them," Lucas said. "What about you?"

"To be honest? No, I don't want children," Sam said, feeling a flush heat her face at the admission. "Which may be horrible to say as a woman, but that's the truth. I think it's because I didn't have a very happy upbringing. Or perhaps I'm just not maternal."

"Judging by the way you're sneaking Pipin chicken and smothering him with love, I wouldn't say you're not maternal." Lucas laughed when Sam flashed him a guilty look.

"Sorry. Should I not feed him from the table?"

"It's fine. You've made a friend for life now," Lucas said, leaning back to pat his belly, which had Sam ogling his bare chest again. "I don't think it's horrible to not want children. I'd say it's better you know yourself than to bring a child into this world if you don't want to be a mother."

"Thank you for that. I wish other people in my life would see that I don't want the same things they do," Sam ground out. She sipped her tea, the cool liquid seeming to soothe the burn of resentment a bit.

"Ah, your parents pushing you to have kids?"

"They push me to do everything they want," Sam said.

"Hm, that doesn't sound fun. Want to tell me about it?" Lucas asked.

Sam found that she did, actually, want to tell him about it. She gave him a quick run-through of how they'd dominated her life choices and used guilt as a tool to keep her in line.

"Just from a casual observation, that almost sounds abusive or toxic," Lucas said, his tone gentle.

Sam's mouth dropped open. "Oh… no. No. They just want what's best for me," Sam said, honestly shocked at his perception of things.

"They want you to fall in line with their demands. When you step outside the norm or tell them that you're not going to do what they want, they tell you to 'have a nice life.' Wouldn't you say that's a little emotionally manipulative? Like a child stomping their feet and having a tantrum until you give in to what they want? It's extremely controlling and plays on your emotions. Even more telling is that you're sitting here feeling guilty and defending them. All in all, I'd say that's quite the mind fuck they've pulled on you."

"I…" Sam was a bit shocked at his harsh assessment, but let it sit with her a moment. "Well, I honestly don't know what to say. I've never looked at it like that before."

"Unconditional love should be just that – without conditions. It shouldn't be only given if orders are followed. You're a grown woman, Samantha. You have every right to make choices for yourself, that you feel are best for you, and expect your family to support you. That's normal," Lucas said.

"You're right. I'm a little bit embarrassed to say it, but you're absolutely right. I can't believe I've been living under this for so long. It's not like I'm a bad person or doing dumb things with my life. But I just want to be able to make those choices – myself. Even if I screw it up. At the very least, I'll have learned from it, you know?" Sam shrugged a shoulder and turned back to her plate. She was surprised to realize she'd eaten everything on her plate.

"So what's stopping you now?" Lucas asked.

Sam found herself grinning at him, feeling a newfound power slip through her. She wondered if this was the inner mermaid power Irma had instructed her to find. Whatever it was, it felt great.

"Absolutely nothing," Sam said, and stood.

CHAPTER 22

"I'll clean the plates, you just relax." Lucas immediately stood as well, but Sam ignored his words and went over to stand in front of him. Looking up, she pressed a hand to his chest and smiled.

"What if I don't want to relax?"

"Vacations are meant for relaxing," Lucas said, his tone light though his look had sharpened.

"Will you kiss me again? Like last night?" Sam said, feeling nerves skitter through her stomach. She wished she could be like Lola or Jolie and just grab the man's head and kiss him breathless.

"It's all I've been thinking about," Lucas admitted, sending heat racing straight through her core as he lowered his head and brushed his lips over hers, once, twice, and then lingered.

Sam's eyes drifted closed as she leaned into him, tasting pineapple and something deeper – more elemental – on his lips. The leaves of the palms fluttered overhead, the breeze bringing with it the scent of salt from the waves that crashed gently on the beach below. For a second, the world drifted away, and nothing mattered but this moment and this man.

She wanted to feel free. To start over – to do something right now that she could clasp to her heart and hold in her memory, to be taken out on those long boring days at work and relived with bittersweet angst. Sliding her hands up his chest, she marveled at the feel of him, sun-warmed skin and hard muscles under her palms, and she was delighted to find that she wanted to follow the trail of her hands with her mouth. Pulling back, Sam shot him a glance from beneath her lids before reaching up on her tiptoes and beginning to press kisses down his neck.

Lucas let out a breath and Sam was shocked to realize that the man was fighting to hold onto his control.

Because of her. She was doing that to him.

And if the hardness pressed against her stomach was any indication, Lucas was anything but bored with her. Enthralled, Sam continued to explore his body with her hands, trailing her hands over the carved muscles in his arms, then back down his chest to toy daringly with the tie of his board shorts. At her touch, he grabbed both of her wrists in his hands and pulled them away from his shorts, devouring her mouth with a kiss that seared its way straight to her brain.

"Sam," he gasped against her mouth.

"Lucas," Sam said, laughing at him.

"You make it hard to want to take it slow with you. I promised myself I would take it slow," Lucas said, still holding her wrists tight. Sam found that being unable to touch him only made her want him more.

"Nobody said you had to take it slowly," Samantha argued, biting his lower lip in frustration.

"You're the kind of girl who needs to take it slow," Lucas said.

Samantha almost stamped her foot in frustration. "That makes me sound like a boring fuddy-duddy," she groused.

"Trust me, you are anything but boring," Lucas laughed down at her, still holding her hands. "But I want to let you bloom – to let Siren Island work its magic on you. That takes time, and trust."

"I…" Sam licked her lips and Lucas narrowed his eyes, bending to kiss where she had just licked. "I don't know if I want you to take it slow. I'm nervous and I think I need you to just push me past that."

"I'll never push a woman," Lucas said. "And we will get where we both want this to go. But, you see… there's this thing they say about island time."

"What's that?" Sam said, a haze of lust clouding her thinking. The man had just admitted he wanted her in bed.

"See, on the island, we like to take things nice and slow. There's no rush to get anywhere, you understand?

Small pleasures are meant to be enjoyed," Lucas said, nudging her backward until she felt the brush of the hammock swing hit the back of her knees. Carefully, Lucas lowered Sam until she sat, rocking gently in the hammock and staring directly at… well, she blushed and looked back up at him.

"So, you're telling me no?" Sam asked, trying to focus on what he was saying.

"I'm saying that I'm going to seduce you, Samantha Jameson. Nice and slow, until all you can think about is being with me – us together – when we're both ready," Lucas said, and Sam's stomach dropped when he knelt between her legs. His hands brushed lightly across her breasts, toying with the strings to her bikini top. Sam wanted to scream – she felt like she would explode if he didn't take her soon. The stress of life, everything, seemed to just fill her up and she wanted to, for one moment, forget it all.

Seeming to sense the frustration radiating from her, Lucas shocked her by untying the bottom of her bikini as he trailed kisses up her leg.

"Now, lay back, look up at the sky, and let me do things my way – nice and slow," Lucas said.

Samantha gulped and then suppressed a nervous giggle when his mouth found the spot where she wanted him most. Shocked, Samantha leaned back in the hammock, throwing an arm over her head and doing exactly as he told her to. It didn't take long before the heat built deep inside of her and it was all almost too much for her. The press of his mouth, the gentle sway of the hammock, the soft play of the sunlight that filtered through the palm trees – it all combined to have Sam teetering on the brink in moments.

Even though she wanted to prolong the sensation, Sam found she couldn't wait any more and tipped over the edge into exquisite bliss – a gift from a man who expected nothing from her, asked for nothing in return. As the final waves of pleasure rippled through her, Sam pulled her arm from above her head and glanced shyly down at a grinning Lucas.

"I… I don't know what to say," Sam said, words failing her.

"Say, 'Thank you, Lucas, that was lovely,'" Lucas decided, smiling devilishly as he pulled her to standing. She gasped and grabbed at the strings of her bikini to tie it back around her hip.

"Thank you, Lucas. Can I… um…" Sam blushed again, wishing she wasn't so awkward with this stuff.

"Cuddle with me in the hammock for a siesta? Absolutely," Lucas said, surprising her, as he pulled her toward a longer hammock tucked between two palms in the shade. In moments, he'd deposited her next to him so that her head nestled on his chest and his arm was wrapped around her. Sam squirmed against him a bit, setting the hammock rocking, and found she couldn't keep the silly smile from her face.

"You do that, um, well," Sam finally said, glancing up at Lucas as he chuckled. Bending down a little, he brushed a kiss against her lips, then gave her a searing look.

"I want you to look at me the next time we're together and remember where my mouth has been and the pleasure I've given you," Lucas said, his eyes hot on hers.

"Oh my," Sam gasped and buried her head against his chest as he chuckled once more, the vibration of his laughter rumbling in his chest.

As afternoons went, Sam thought before she drifted off, it was one for the books.

CHAPTER 23

"You did what?" Lola screeched into the phone so loudly the next morning that Samantha had to hold the phone away from her ear. Sam had to admit, it felt good to be the one who had a deliciously naughty story to tell for once.

"You heard me," Samantha said, bending over to apply another coat of red polish to her toes. Turning the bottle over, she checked the name – Siren. Squinting, Sam thought about when she'd bought this bottle. About a week before the trip, she was at a store picking up antacids and had seen it displayed on a little rack by the checkout. Typically, Sam stayed with neutral colors, but had picked the bottle up on impulse and tossed it in her basket. Had she noticed the name at the time, she wondered? Was that the subliminal message that had added an extra boost for her to book this trip? Either way, Sam was beginning to think it was one of the best decisions she'd made in years.

"I am in awe. Shock and awe over here," Lola said, "And so damn proud of you. I like this new Samantha. I know you have a lot going on in your head and a whole lot of real life to deal with, but I am so proud of you for letting go, even if it's just for a little bit, and letting yourself live life a little on the wild side."

"Lola, I have a confession to make," Sam said, making her voice serious.

"Oh no, what did you do?" Lola breathed.

"I think I might like it on the wild side," Sam said and laughed when Lola cheered again.

"You know what I like about this guy? That he napped with you after. I mean… that says something, doesn't it?"

"That he was tired?" Sam asked, keeping her tone light. She didn't want – no, she *refused* to look any deeper into this situation with Lucas. The clock was ticking on her time on Siren Island. It wouldn't do for her to get too attached to him.

"No, silly. That he wanted more than to just get his and go. He lingered with you. Snuggled you in. The man wants to protect you and get to know the real you. I'm telling you, Sam, don't turn your back on this one," Lola advised.

"What? This coming from Miss Love 'Em and Leave 'Em?" Sam laughed, stretching her foot out to admire her toes.

"And there's a damn good reason I do leave them. I'm not ready for a long-term relationship. So I pick men that I know will be a diversion for a while. We both know what we're in it for – so nobody's heart gets hurt. Mutual affection and enjoyment. That's the name of the game," Lola said.

"So? I'd say Lucas and I have mutual affection." Sam shrugged, trying to play it cool.

"Sam, come on. As long as I've known you, you've never been one to pull off casual affairs. And I don't think you should try to with this guy. He cooked you lunch, counseled you on your toxic family, gave you the best orgasm of your life, and then cuddled you in a hammock. And!" Lola cut Sam off when she was about to speak. "And he's got a cute dog. I mean, *be still* my heart."

"Pipin is pretty damn cute," Sam agreed.

"Just… okay, can you just promise me one thing?" Lola asked.

"Depends what it is," Sam said.

"Promise you won't try to poke holes in this or look for all the things wrong with it or reasons why it couldn't work. I'm not saying get your head in the clouds and picture walking down the aisle with this man. But, just… can you just give it a chance? And see what happens?" Lola asked.

"You want me to believe in a fairy tale?"

"I want you to believe that happy endings can look

different from what's been carefully mapped out and planned for you," Lola said.

Sam winced at the truth of the words. "That's fair," she said.

"Good. Now, tell me – what are your plans for the day?"

"Don't yell at me, but I'm going to check in with work," Sam said, and now it was her turn to cut off Lola's protestations. "Lola, stop. It's my job and it's me. It's who I am. I can't shake being responsible. I promise to not get sucked into any problems, but I do need to check in with accounts. Then after that Lucas is going to take me for an adventure around the island, he said. Maybe snorkeling? I'm not sure, but he told me to wear my bikini again."

"Eeeek!" Lola shrieked.

Sam laughed, shaking her head at the phone. "I'm hanging up now," she said.

"Don't forget to shave your legs!"

Sam laughed down at the phone and then pulled her laptop open. Thus far she'd successfully avoided addressing any work emails, but it had been a real challenge. It was deeply ingrained in her to check her phone constantly and to review any emails, or handle any issues that arose, as quickly as possible. Scanning the several pages of emails that awaited her, Sam took a deep breath and began to do something she hadn't done for most of her tenure at Paradiso.

Delegate.

In an hour, she'd assigned, answered, or handled everything that was needed – then, because she knew she could be sucked in further as people began to respond to her being online, she put up a vacation autoresponder for the first time ever.

Now *that* felt good.

Sam stood and stretched, closing her laptop and plugging it in on the sideboard. Glancing at the clock, she jumped. She only had a half hour to get ready, and she'd promised Lucas she'd get snacks for their adventure.

Sam snorted indelicately at the word 'adventure.' It was ridiculous, really, that she was off for an adventure day. It was more of an outing or an excursion, she thought as she stepped under the spray of the shower and quickly shaved as Lola had advised. Toweling off, Sam glanced in the mirror and raised her eyebrows at the tousle of curls that rioted around her face. There was no use trying to straighten and tame that mess of hair in this humidity. Best to embrace it; maybe one of these days Jolie or Mirra would teach her to braid it like they did.

Slipping on her red bikini, a little sliver of pleasure sliced through her as she remembered Lucas untying the bikini bottom. It had just been so… decadent. Something she never would have allowed herself to indulge in before, Sam mused, as she pulled one of her new cover-ups, a deep azure trimmed with little discs of shiny gold, over her head. She wouldn't say she'd been a prude – at least not with Noah she hadn't been – but she was the private sort. Outdoor sex of any kind had always been off the table. And here she'd just laid out for a man in a hammock on his patio.

Settling her new necklace over her head and tossing on some long dangly earrings – far more exotic than she'd ever wear in a corporate environment – Sam glanced once more in the mirror. It was like she was looking at a different person. Her eyes seemed to glow in her face, her hair was wild around her head, and she was dripping gold shimmers – and was that… joy? Serenity? Sam didn't know this woman yet, but she'd like to.

CHAPTER 24

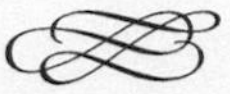

It wasn't Irma she found in the kitchen, but Jolie and Mirra – and Samantha was immediately submitted to an inquisition that would rival the ancient Spaniards.

"Mama said you spent the day with Lucas yesterday," Jolie said, hand on hip. Today she wore pink – an intricately crocheted dress that hugged every inch of her curves.

"And came back smiling," Mirra added from where she stirred something on the stove. She wore the palest shade of yellow today, in the form of flowy pants and a barely-there halter top.

"Are you this nosy with all your guests?" Sam wondered.

"Yes," Jolie admitted, reaching up to pull a wicker picnic basket from the cabinet.

"Just the ones we like," Mirra demurred, tossing a smile at Sam over her shoulder.

"Tell us everything," Jolie demanded, putting the picnic basket on the table and going to the industrial-size refrigerator that dominated one side of the room.

"Well, maybe not everything. She's the private sort, Jolie. How about just a little tidbit?" Mirra asked.

Sam briefly wondered how these two women had such a good read on her, considering they barely knew her, and then gave up. She slid onto a chair at the kitchen counter as the women bustled about, putting together a basket of food for her adventure day with Lucas. Sam still almost giggled every time she thought about having an adventure.

"He's an amazing kisser," Sam said with a devilish smile, and the women sighed.

"I just knew it," Jolie announced as she sliced up cheese for the basket. "He has that look about him, you know? A man who can kiss well carries himself with confidence."

"You've never tested those waters?" Sam asked, keeping her voice casual but desperately wanting to know. If Jolie and Mirra were her competition, then she was out of luck. Those two were seriously gorgeous.

"He's not for us," Mirra said, shaking her blonde hair as she laughed. "Not that we can't appreciate a good-looking man. We already told you he was just our friend."

"I know, I guess I just have a hard time believing it.

You all live so close together, and you're all so damn good-looking," Sam grumbled.

"I think there was a compliment in there somewhere," Jolie preened as she tossed her curls.

"I'm sorry, that was rude of me," Sam said immediately.

"No need to apologize." Mirra smiled gently.

"We agree, though," Jolie laughed. "We are damn good-looking. And so is that man of yours. But the whole living close to each other… Well, sometimes it's best not to muddy the waters. Living on an island is like living in a very small town. Everybody is extremely interested in everyone else's business. You're smart to keep your mouth shut and gossip about nobody – and when you do decide to, uh, dance with a man, choose carefully."

"I never thought about it like that," Sam said. "I'm so used to living in a big city."

"Life's different down here. The last thing you want is to have a fling with a neighbor and then have to live next to him for years," Mirra said.

"And watch him bring home a slew of new women," Jolie all but growled.

Sam raised an eyebrow. "Is this from experience then?"

"Another time, another place." Jolie waved it away and pasted a bright smile back on her beautiful face. "But rest easy, my friend. Lucas is all yours. We'll just live vicariously through you – but only if you're not greedy with the details."

"I've never had anyone live vicariously through me," Sam mused, peeking into the ever-growing pile of food that was being deposited into the picnic basket.

"No? I thought you said you traveled a ton for work. I'm sure some people you know envied that?" Mirra asked.

"I… well, hmm," Sam said, tilting her head as she thought about it, "Perhaps people wanted to live vicariously through me in what they assumed my life was like. But reality is hardly the stuff of daydreams."

"It can be," Jolie said, flipping the basket top closed and latching it.

"I mean… sure, I guess. But not really. You still have to work and all that." Sam shrugged.

"But work should give you pleasure," Mirra said.

"And you should live where you want." Jolie swung the basket easily from the counter.

"And love who you want," Mirra added as they headed for the door.

"And dress how you want," Jolie said, pointing at her pink crochet dress.

"Okay, okay – I get it." Sam raised both hands, laughing. These two would make her head spin. They were like life coaches on speed – and she had to admit their pep talks were very effective. Primarily because they left little room for talking about anything other than what they were drilling into her brain. "So, just daydream what I want my life to be and it'll turn into that."

"Exactly," Jolie said, surprising Sam with a kiss to her cheek, so delighted was she with Sam's assessment.

"I'm not sure it really works like that," Sam said, as the three of them left the kitchen to go out front of the villa to wait for Lucas's 4-runner.

"Sure it does," Mirra said, waving at Lucas as he beeped his approach. "You manifest your reality. Your words, your thoughts, your actions. Dreams can be as real as you want them to be – if you believe in them."

"Yeah, but… you can dream about winning the lottery all you want, but that might not happen." Sam's logical side couldn't help but rear its head.

"Ah, sure. But people only dream of winning the lottery to ease some of their current tensions. It could be credit card debt, a mortgage, or work stress. However, winning the lottery isn't the only solution to those issues. So if the dream is to have the money to resolve whatever the stresses may be, it might not come via the lottery, but the person can still manifest an answer," Jolie said. She turned to hand the picnic basket to Lucas. "Hey there, handsome. Taking our pretty guest on an adventure?"

"Sure am, and I have to say you're all looking lovely today," Lucas said.

Jolie and Mirra positively glowed under his words, shaking their curls and pressing kisses to his cheeks. It would have made her jealous if Sam weren't beginning to understand that this was just their way. These women were happy, enthusiastic about life, and loving. It seemed they embraced everything with joy, and she had yet to see any sign that either of them had a mean bone in their bodies.

"Thanks for putting the basket together for me," Sam said. She was showered with the same amount of hugs and kisses as Lucas had received, then the sisters waved them on their way.

"Remember, it's a small island," Jolie whispered in her ear before she let Sam out of her hug. "If you do something too naughty in a public place, we'll all know."

Sam blanched white as she thought about the day before. Pulling back, Jolie assessed her face and laughed, touching the tip of Sam's nose with her finger.

"Don't worry, we live on a private beach. Have fun, you two!"

"You look beautiful today," Lucas said, surprising Sam by pulling her to him and lingering over a kiss until they both heard catcalls from the doorway. "Just giving them what they wanted."

"Is that all it was?" Sam asked, half aroused and half annoyed, as she slid onto the dusty seat of his beat-up truck.

"And to make sure you weren't nervous about seeing me again after yesterday," Lucas said cheerfully as Sam blushed.

"I'm not nervous," Sam insisted.

“You’ve got nervous-type written all over you, sweets. I’d say five minutes away from the house you’d have started stuttering and trying to work yourself past the awkwardness you feel about yesterday.”

“I’m not nervous about it.” Sam narrowed her eyes at him behind her sunglasses. “I’ll have you know I quite enjoyed it, thank you very much.”

“I know you did.” Lucas shot her a shit-eating grin and she dissolved into laughter.

“I walked right into that, didn’t I?”

“Hey, a man likes his ego flattered, you know?” Lucas laughed and Sam felt the tension ease from her shoulders. Damn if the man wasn’t right – she had been nervous about seeing him again.

“All right, Captain. Take me on an adventure.”

“You don’t have to ask me twice,” Lucas said, and gunned the engine.

CHAPTER 25

"It always helps to explore the island with a local," Lucas said as he turned the truck away from the direction of town.

"Is that what you are now? A local?" Sam murmured, leaning a hand out the window to catch the breeze as they rumbled past a row of palms tucked on a cliff wall by the sea. "That has such a nice ring to it. Usually at home we'll tell people where we're from or that we grew up here, but I rarely say I'm a local."

"I do like the terminology, I'll admit. It gives a sense of belonging, I suppose," Lucas mused. "Or maybe a badge of honor? Since island life isn't always as easy as it seems."

"How so? I mean, I know we talked about trading problems the other day – but what do you find to be particularly difficult?" Sam asked, tapping her hand to the beat of the reggae music he had turned on low.

"Mmm, it's a mix of things, I suppose. We don't Amazon Prime items to our doorstep every day. So we have to make do with what we have or wait weeks or months for new parts to arrive. That makes most islanders a blend of hoarders and handymen. You have to learn to be self-sufficient, build it or patch it yourself, and when you see an item you love – buy all of it."

Sam laughed and then realized he was serious.

"Buy all of it? Like what?"

"Your favorite brand of beer? Buy all the cases. Your favorite cereal? Buy all the boxes. Favorite soap? Buy it all," Lucas said, shifting gears and directing the truck up a steep incline. Sam held on as they bounced through some ruts in the dirt road. "Shops don't automatically restock when an item is sold out. Or if they do, it might not be the same brand. I have an entire pantry and freezer full of favorite items."

"I… wow, I never thought about it like that."

"We have Facebook groups. It's not uncommon for someone to post, 'what shop has bananas for sale today?' and have everyone chime in to let them know if there are bananas on island."

"That's amazing. I guess I just take for granted that I can get what I want when I go to the grocery store," Sam mused.

"And now apply that to everything – underwear, computer equipment, car parts and so on. It's not to say that you can't find these things, but sometimes you either have to track it down, make do with what you find, or wait a month or two for your online order to come in."

"I suppose that cuts down on some impulse shopping." Sam thought of the embarrassing number of times she had clicked "Order Now" on her Amazon account.

"It does. But you don't need as much here either. You spend a large part of your day outside, so shoes are optional. Clothing is fairly casual on an island, and pretty much everyone drives a run-down car."

"I noticed that about the cars," Sam said, eyeing his dust-covered dashboard with the air conditioner that struggled to let out little puffs of cool air, even though they had the windows open.

"It doesn't make sense to buy a fancy car. First of all, they're all wired with fancy electronics now. When one wire corrodes in this salt air, it's all gone. And nobody will have the part for it. Since the salt air and humidity gets to everything eventually, why waste the money? Not to mention the goats." Lucas slanted her a look.

"Shut up!" Sam said, smacking him lightly on the arm as she laughed.

"I am dead serious when I say I've come outside to see goats standing on the hood of my car. Look," Lucas gestured.

Samantha peered through the windshield, where she could make out little divots in the hood of the truck.

"Why were they standing on your truck?" Sam gasped.

"To eat the bushes that are higher up," Lucas laughed.

"Naturally," Sam said.

"But the tradeoff for these things is this – just look," Lucas said, and pulled the car to the side of the dirt road as they reached the top of the cliff.

Sam gasped – the world seemed to open up in front of them. Unable to help herself, she hopped from the car and went to stand at the edge of the cliff. Jagged edges of cliff wall jutted out below her, seeming to thrust directly from the depths of the turquoise blue water. From here, the whole island seemed to spread out before her and she could see the tiny colorful buildings of the village hugging the harbor, fishing boats lazily cruising the water, and even a few windmills standing tall on the other side of the island. The island, which she'd first perceived as flat when her plane had landed, was anything but. It rolled and curved, dipped and dived, and had its own stark beauty of desert cactuses and proud palm trees. But the sea – oh, the sea called to her.

From here she could look out for miles, with nothing to obscure her view, and see what seemed like a million shades of blue. On the horizon, waves tipped over into little splashes of white. The water shifted and moved, and the more she watched it, the more she seemed to see.

"It's why I moved here," Lucas said, coming to stand next to her, his shoulder pressing into hers.

"It's like looking into Mother Nature's soul. Look at this gift she's showing us," Samantha breathed, and Lucas looped his arm easily around her shoulders, pulling her gently into him so that her arm naturally went around his waist.

"It's different. Every day it's different. She shifts and tumbles about and gets mad or cheerful. I'm constantly amazed at the many moods of the ocean. I never tire of it," Lucas said.

"Thanks for bringing me up here," Sam said, looking up at him, her eyes tracing his strong jawline.

When he glanced down at her, it seemed the most natural thing in the world that he would bend and press a kiss to her lips.

Something shimmered in the air around them, and Sam felt it once again, like the night he'd been telling the story of the mermaids. The weight of it pressed against her skin and her heart seemed to whisper, Why not this one?

Why not, she wondered, as she pulled away and turned to look back out at the water. She tilted her head, seeing a flash of something far out on the water. The fanciful part of her brain perked up immediately: A mermaid's tail! Then she smiled and shook her head a bit; in all reality it was probably just a fish.

"What?" Lucas asked.

"I just thought I saw something in the water is all," Samantha laughed.

"Could have. Fish jump, and dolphins are often spotted off the coast here."

"Oh, dolphins! That would be fun to see," Sam gushed.

"Well, hopefully I'll be able to deliver them to you at our next spot. Ready to move on?"

Sam glanced balefully at him and stuck her lip out in an exaggerated pout.

"Do we have to?"

"Yes, unless you want to sunburn that pretty skin of yours. It gets hot up here near midday, and there's no shade."

"I suppose if I must go." Samantha sighed and glanced once more out at the horizon before turning back to the truck.

"Don't worry, I'll bring you back here any time you want. How about a sunset date one night? It feels like you're on top of the world," Lucas said, brushing a hand down her arm.

"I'd like that," Sam said, trying not to do the thing where she poked holes in all the things that could be wrong with this man. She reminded herself to just sit back and enjoy.

She'd promised Lola, after all.

CHAPTER 26

Samantha could barely keep the smile off her face as Lucas navigated the ragged dirt road down the other side of the cliffs. He did his best to avoid the potholes while Sam kept up a steady stream of chatter, exclaiming over the things she saw.

"I'm surprised you like this so much," Lucas laughed at her.

"Why?" Sam demanded.

"Because you've traveled all over the world for your job. I feel like you've seen loads of beautiful places," Lucas said.

"Well, I mean, I have. But most of them – at least where Paradiso properties are located – are just so…" Samantha tapped her lips as she thought about the right word. "They're very manicured. You don't get rough and undeveloped like this. Which, sometimes, is when you have the most beauty, no?"

"I agree," Lucas said, shooting her a small smile. "Rough around the edges can be really beautiful. I think Siren Island blends that well. We have enough modern amenities to meet our needs, and yet we have loads of wild spaces that haven't been bulldozed by large hotel chains and Americanized. I hope it stays this way always."

"My company would be one of the ones to bulldoze this beach," Sam said, feeling sad as she realized the truth of it. Usually she never saw properties until they were finished and occupied. Approving a building budget or managing rental income portfolios kept her looking at spreadsheets all day; she was never really exposed to what an area looked like prior to a build.

"How does that make you feel?" Lucas asked, being diplomatic though she could imagine his thoughts. He'd pulled the truck beneath the shade of a few straggly palm trees, and they sat for a moment, looking out at the ocean before them.

"Sad," Sam said, turning to look at him. "I'm so far removed from that aspect of it that I rarely think about the impact it has on the communities or the environment around it. I suppose I've always been taught that tourism is good for places and that everyone welcomes tourist dollars. I forget what that can destroy, as well. Though I did spearhead one environmental campaign I'm very proud of," Sam said, as they both opened their doors to get out.

"What's that?" Lucas asked, swinging a cooler over

one arm, hooking two beach chairs over the other, and then grabbing the picnic basket with his free hand before she could reach for it. Even though it was such a man thing to do – like getting home from the grocery store and refusing to make two trips to carry the bags in from the car – the effect of seeing him carrying everything made her a bit giddy.

"I watched a documentary called *Chasing Coral* and it made me realize how horrible sunscreens are – not only for your skin and your own health, but for the ocean as well. Though my boss got a little annoyed with me, I pushed a company-wide policy through so that only reef-safe sunscreen could be sold at any of our resorts and properties. Ultimately, the good press we got appeased my boss, but I'm just happy that I could make a bit of a difference."

"That's awesome!" Lucas's smile was wide on his face as he led her down a path strewn with gravel and bits of shells toward a makeshift palapa that had been constructed from fallen palm fronds. "You should be really proud of yourself. You'd be amazed what a difference that can make."

"Thanks, I appreciate that," Sam laughed, feeling warm inside from his praise. "Everyone at work thought I was a bit silly, especially tucked away in the middle of the States like we are, but hey – I figured it was worth trying."

"And the ocean thanks you for it," Lucas said, bending to put the chairs down beneath the palapa and dropping the baskets in the sand. “As do I. So are you ready to see what kind of difference you’ve made?”

“What?” Sam tilted her head at him.

“Out there? Ready for a snorkel? I’ll show you some of the pretty reefs you’ve had a hand in saving,” Lucas said.

Sam looked around, worry lacing through her. They were on a completely deserted beach, with not a house, human being, or boat anywhere to be seen. What if there were currents? Or a shark bit them? There was nobody to help. How fast could an emergency vehicle get here? Were there emergency vehicles on the island?

“Is there… like a designated swim area? How do you know where to go? Is there a lifeguard?” Sam stammered, looking around again. The waves went from friendly-looking to menacing in her eyes.

“I promise I’ll take care of you. I even have a pool noodle in the car for you to float on if you’re not a strong swimmer,” Lucas said, stepping over to rub his hands up and down her arms.

“I just… I’m not used to plunging into water where there’s nobody around to call for help, I guess. It’s just so… I feel like I’m on a deserted island here,” Sam said, looking up at him.

“I’m CPR certified, I’m a rescue diver, I have a phone here that I can use to radio for help, and I promise not to take you anywhere that has heavy currents. I know this bay and these reefs really well,” Lucas said.

“Okay… I trust you,” Sam said, but she assumed her

look said anything but, because he threw back his head and laughed.

"If you hate it, tell me and I'll bring you in right away. But I suspect you'll be so distracted by the underwater aquarium before your eyes that you'll forget about your nerves right away."

"Let's do this then," Sam said.

Lucas pulled a mask and snorkel from his bag, showing her how to fit it to her face and how to keep her hair from making the mask leak.

"I suspect this isn't my sexiest look," Samantha said around the snorkel in her mouth and Lucas laughed at her again and took the mask off her.

"I think you look very adventurous," he teased.

Even though he was teasing, it made Sam feel good inside to be thought of as adventurous. This was what all the people who were jealous of her job thought she was doing when she was traveling all the time – not sitting inside conference rooms. She kicked off her flip-flops, pulled off her coverup, and deposited her jewelry on top of it, making a little pile on the chair.

"Will our stuff be safe here–"

The breath left her as Lucas whirled her to him, devouring her lips in a slick open-mouthed kiss that flashed lust straight down to her toes. Briefly, she remembered the phrase "making her toes curl" before he took her under once more. She gasped against his lips, suddenly hungry for more. She'd always laughed at the saying, but now, as she curled her toes into the sand to try and brace against the onslaught that was Lucas and the need that raced desperately through her, she finally understood it.

Breathing heavily, Lucas broke the kiss and pressed his forehead to hers.

"Uh… wow," Sam said.

"I'm sorry, I'm doing my best to be a gentleman. But I've been dying to do that since I saw you walk out of the villa today. You looked like a tropical parrot, laughing in your colorful dress with the other two girls. It was like a painting of beautiful bright women, and it just lit me up inside knowing that I got to have you as my date today."

Sam released a long slow breath, and smiled up at him even as her brain churned. Damn it, Lola was right. She might not be built for one-night stands. Because if he kept talking to her like this, Samantha was certain she'd fall for him.

Which could be a very dangerous mistake for her heart.

"I'm really happy to be here with you," Sam said, feeling shy. She wanted to be as open with her feelings as he was being, but couldn't quite bring herself to let her walls down. "Everything about this feels surreal – like an enchantment."

"Well, then, let me continue the fairy tale and invite you to my enchanted reef." Lucas bowed gallantly –

well, as gallantly as he could with his arms full of snorkel gear – and Sam fought to keep the silly grin from her face.

"I'd be delighted."

CHAPTER 27

It really was like an aquarium, Sam thought, after she got past her initial nervousness. Not to mention the initial flooding of her mask and subsequent coughing fit that had Lucas patting her on the back to help her out. And she wasn't going to even think about when she had tripped in her fins at the edge of the water before Lucas tugged her to his side and showed her that walking backward in fins made more sense. Nope, she wasn't going to think about that at all, Sam decided as she floated next to Lucas. He'd hooked his arm loosely through hers and intertwined his hand with hers. It was silly that such a simple and sweet gesture would pull at her heartstrings so.

There was so much to see! Sam's eyes darted back and forth, trying to track all the sea life that flitted past her face. After the first few times she'd brought her head up to ask questions about the fish and subsequently swallowed a mouthful of seawater, Lucas had ordered her to just relax and look at everything. He'd brought along a nifty little water camera and had promised her he'd take pictures and answer all her questions after. Once that promise was secured, Sam felt more comfortable relaxing and just looking at the stunning dance of life that spread out before her.

It was like a movie, she decided, where everyone had their own little part. Small schools of baby silver fish darted close to them, while a large rainbow-colored fish seemed to take bites out of the actual reef. A pair of black and gold fish almost in a flat triangle shape sailed past them, turning to look at them with eyes that looked to be ringed in gold eyeliner. Lucas made a halo motion above his forehead and she wondered what he'd meant, but stayed true to her promise to just float and watch everything.

Sea fans waved in the gentle surge of the water, and corals in every color imaginable created a reef system where crabs scuttled to hide from them and black fish darted out at them as if to warn them away from their personal coral real estate. When a long slimy green thing poked its head from a hole, Sam clutched Lucas's hand. She was pretty sure it was an eel and she knew they could bite. But Lucas just tugged her along, kicking them over the eel – which opened its mouth at them, looking for all the world like he was laughing at his own private joke. Sam found herself giggling into her mask at the thought.

Lucas squeezed her hand once more, motioning excitedly in front of her face and Sam turned to see a large green turtle swimming lazily along the bottom. Her heart squeezed in her chest as she watched the sunlight play through the water, its beams dappling against the turtle's shell, and she was surprised to feel her eyes slick with tears as he swam straight to the surface in front of her. He was so close she could have reached out and touched him. Instead she hung there, floating with Lucas as the turtle gulped air and turned to eye them. Deciding they were no threat, he hung around for a moment before diving deep back into the ocean, careening gently across the ocean floor, looking for his next spot to nestle into.

It was amazing, this world that Lucas was showing her. For the first time in her life, Samantha fell well and truly in love with something – and it was the peace she felt here, floating in this water, with nobody demanding anything of her other than that she take joy in the beauty around her.

A flash of silver caught her eye and Sam turned, once again feeling like she saw something out of the corner of her eye. When a large tail fin flitted out of the depths, she pulled Lucas instinctively closer, and charged forward as fast as she could in fins she wasn't used to using. She had to see… there was something, just *something* outside the line of her vision disappearing off into the blue.

When Lucas tugged her hand, forcing her to look at

him, he raised an eyebrow at her, but she just shrugged her shoulders. Maybe she was imagining things. She must have just gotten too caught up in the moment and her mind ran away with possibilities, she supposed.

Then the glint of something on the ocean floor caught her eye. Tilting her head, she pointed down to it. Lucas looked at it, then back at her, making a stop motion with his hand. For a moment, when he let go of her hand, Samantha's heart picked up its beat as she realized she might have pulled them further out than they should be. What if a current swept them away? Forcing herself to breathe slowly, she watched as Lucas dove neatly down to the ocean floor and collected the item, tucking it in the pocket of his cargo shorts. Ascending, he hooked her hand once more and swam them gently toward shore.

Once she could stand, Sam popped her head from the water, launching herself at a startled Lucas. He had barely pulled his mask off before she'd wrapped her arms and legs around his waist, and kissed him as thoroughly as he'd kissed her before they'd gone in the ocean. His hands automatically cupped her bottom, and Sam shivered against him, wanting more. She nibbled at his bottom lip, almost delirious with sensations that threatened to overwhelm her.

"I take it you enjoyed that?" Lucas panted against her lips as he held her while the water lapped gently around them.

"It was the most beautiful thing I've ever seen. Can

we do it again? After lunch? I want more. I can't believe it – there's so much to see!" Samantha gasped with excitement, though she wasn't sure if it was over the man or the ocean or both.

"We can go as much as you'd like," Lucas laughed. "We can even get you scuba certified if you're comfortable with it."

"Scuba? Shut up," Sam said in delight, squeezing his shoulder muscles under her hands. "Yes, please. That sounds like something an adventurous person would do."

"Then let's get you signed up for your open water course," Lucas said, letting her slide down his body. She sighed as she lost contact with him, but then thought back to what she had seen in the water.

"What was the fish eating the reef? I swear I could hear it take a bite," Sam asked as they walked to the palapa where their stuff was.

"Parrot fish. They eat the reef and then poop it out as sand," Lucas said cheerfully.

Sam stopped in her tracks, staring down at the sand between her toes. "You're saying I'm standing in fish poop," she demanded, convinced he was pulling her leg.

"Correct. Cool, huh?"

"That's such a guy thing to think is cool," Sam decided, taking the towel he handed her and wrapping it around her body before plopping gratefully into one of the low-slung beach chairs. The breeze tickled her face lightly, and the waves continued to lap against the shore, and Sam looked once more at the horizon, searching for… something.

"What did you think you saw when you tugged me out deeper?" Lucas asked, seeming to read her mind.

"I don't quite know. I thought I saw a large fin, or fish, or something. It was really quick – just a flash of light off of scales – and then it was gone. I'm sorry I didn't get a better look, but I couldn't bring myself to swim out any deeper."

"It's smart not to swim too far out if you don't know the water," Lucas agreed, bending to dig around in the cooler.

"What did you pick up off the sand?" Samantha asked as she accepted an ice-cold beer from him. She wasn't typically a beer drinker, but something about the iciness of the beverage and drinking it straight from the bottle felt just right in the heat of midday.

"Oh, right. It looked like a comb," Lucas said, pulling it from his pocket. He studied it for a moment and then handed it over. "It's really pretty, but I have no idea if it's worth anything."

The comb was rounded, and upon closer inspection it looked to be crafted from a shell. Turning it in her hand, Sam gasped at the pearls inlaid on the outside of it in a crescent moon shape.

"It has pearls in it," Sam said, holding it up to show Lucas.

"I saw that. It's pretty, though I'm sure it's not real," Lucas shrugged.

"I don't know, Lucas, this is really fine craftsmanship." Samantha turned the comb over in her hands, studying how the pearls were inlaid in the shell without cracking it.

"Let me see," Lucas said. Plucking it from her hand, he examined it once more before looking up at her. Leaning close, he lifted her chin with one hand so that her eyes met his tawny green ones. With a smile, he slid the comb into her salty hair, which was drying in the ocean breezes.

"There," Lucas said, brushing a kiss over her lips. "You look just like a mermaid."

A hum of power shot through Sam, so deep that she almost dropped her beer. This comb… something about this moment, this comb, this man. Forcing herself to take deep breaths, Samantha willed the thrum of power down inside of her, locking it in her core like a secret to be pulled out later and examined in private. For if she looked too closely at it now, she feared it would shatter into pieces.

CHAPTER 28

Jolie had packed them a feast, Samantha decided, as Lucas unpacked the hamper and set it up on a nifty little table he'd unfolded with the chairs. He hooked a tiny speaker to the back of his chair, and Samantha relaxed into her seat as the island rhythm began to overtake her.

"I could get used to this," Samantha said, taking a sliver of cheese from the board.

"It's not too shabby, right?" Lucas smiled and stretched his long, tanned legs out in front of him in the sand. Damned if she didn't sneak a glance at his ab muscles where they dipped below the waist of his board shorts. Grateful for her sunglasses, Sam raised her bottle of beer at him. Lucas held his up in in response. "Or are you going crazy not being busy all the time?"

"I have to admit, it's taken a serious level of control not to check my phone every two minutes," Samantha said. "But I'm proud of myself. I checked my work email this morning, delegated everything that needed delegating, and then put a vacation responder up for the first time ever in my life. I feel like I passed an important milestone there." She touched the comb at her hair, feeling it hum with an odd vibration she could only attribute to the fact that she was drinking beer at midday on an empty stomach.

"Ah, yes, the first vacation responder email. An important step toward freedom," Lucas said, tapping his beer to hers in cheers.

"Is this your life every day? I mean, sure, when people are in town you probably do this stuff. Not to say this would get boring, but I guess I just can't imagine my life without routine. Or the pressures of a job. I hate to say it, but I'm not sure if I'm cut out for retirement quite yet," Samantha said, "I feel like I'd enjoy it for a bit, but then go a little stir crazy. I think deadlines drive me to be more productive. What do you do with your time? Wasn't it a shock leaving your old job to come to this?"

"Oh, it absolutely was a shock to my system. But, in some respects, I kind of needed it. I really needed the time to grieve my friend. And, I think partly because of how I left work, I initially viewed working as evil. I'd invested well and was able to support myself just fine on what I had in the bank. I spent a lot of time puttering around – diving, exploring, that kind of thing. But, eventually, yeah. I needed to do something. I went back to work." Lucas shrugged and took a swig of his beer.

"You work? What's your boss say about you taking off to go snorkeling in the middle of the week?" Samantha demanded.

"He says so long as it's with a pretty girl, I'm fine." Lucas laughed at her.

"You're the boss, aren't you? What do you do?" Samantha asked, her eyes drawn again to his tanned chest muscles. This was not a man who sat inside at a desk all day, that was for sure.

"It's interesting on an island. A lot of people hodgepodge things, piece it together. I do a little consulting on investments here and there – though once word gets out, you're more in demand than you expect to be. And, for some reason, I invested in a restaurant downtown. I have no idea why – I've never been in the business. But it just felt fun to me. And it has been. I've been more of a silent partner since I have no background in the restaurant business. But there was a local I'd met who had a passion for cooking, the other locals trusted him and wanted to work for him, and together we made a fun little spot downtown. He's as happy as can be being the face of the restaurant and I get to go in and rock in a swing while I eat my food whenever I feel like it."

"The swing restaurant is yours?" Samantha exclaimed. "That was the one place I saw that made me want to forget everything and just relax."

"That's the point of it all, isn't it?" Lucas looked

over at her. "You should savor your food, enjoy it with friends, or just relax and read a book while having a beer. I thought the swings would invite people to feel like children again and just enjoy themselves while partaking of a good local meal."

"You have to take me. I promised myself that when I worked up the gumption to drive that rusty old truck again, I would go there and sit in a swing. I love swings," Samantha said.

"I know. I saw how much you enjoyed mine yesterday," Lucas said, his smile slow and dangerous in his face.

"You're killing me here," Sam said, heat rising to her face. Once again she imagined rolling into cool sheets with him, their skin warm from the sun, the taste of salt on their lips.

"Good, because when we make love, I want your whole world to fall away to just us," Lucas whispered. He reached out to trail a finger down the string of her bikini top, fussing with the neat bow she'd tied at the neck. Slowly he ran his finger up her neck to toy lightly with the curve of her ear, and a shiver shot through her. Lucas grinned – a wicked, naughty bedroom grin – as his gaze dropped to her very visible response through the thin fabric that covered her breasts.

"You are torturing me," Samantha decided.

"It's the best kind of torture," Lucas said, bending over to plop a cheerful kiss on her lips. "Eat up. We may have time for one more snorkel, but we should get home for a siesta before the party tonight."

"There's a party tonight?"

"The ladies are throwing a little beach BBQ. Usually it's just a small group of people for dancing or games on the beach. You'll love it," Lucas said.

How nice was that? Samantha thought. So casual. None of the fussy overly-planned affairs her work and family always scheduled into her calendar. No, just a casual come-as-you-are beach hangout.

"You know what? I think I will."

CHAPTER 29

Lucas took the long loop home, delighting in showing her different areas of the island. It seemed to her that there were little pockets of neighborhoods tucked among the trees and hills all over the island.

"See, each area of the island has its own vibe, and different selling points. Some people like being up on the hill where they catch the trade winds and can look over the island. Others like to be right on the oceanfront, though those properties typically go for a premium. Some of the neighborhoods are clustered close to town where people can walk, bike, or scooter to their jobs. A few neighborhoods consisting almost solely of longtime islanders are further out, away from it all. They try their best to maintain local traditions."

"It's a melting pot," Samantha said, raising an

eyebrow at some newly-built villas that lined one particularly beautiful stretch of the coast. "Those are pretty."

"There's been a push for sustainable eco-tourism. One of the companies that has set up shop here is working on building homes using sustainable practices – solar panels, local materials and furnishings – and gives jobs to the local families. They take the time to teach the trade to people who want to learn, and have been a great addition to the island. Plus, there's a big push for people wanting to stay in smaller eco-friendly areas instead of big all-inclusive hotels. I think they'll do well here," Lucas said as they passed the breezy villas, where workmen were putting the finishing touches on the outside walls.

"It doesn't seem like you have too many hotels," Samantha said.

"We do, but they aren't large like some of the bigger islands that just pile people into all-inclusives like they're just another number or a big cattle herd. The hotels and vacation rentals are smaller here; people come back to visit year after year because the staff stays the same and remembers their names. I think it makes people feel welcome to be recognized on their vacations, you know?"

"I agree. Honestly, it was something I have brought up to Paradiso. I can tell which hotel has a larger turnover of staff just from looking at the accounts to see how many returning guests they have each year."

"You know," Lucas said, sliding a glance at Samantha, "it sounds like you're pretty good at your job."

"Thanks, I try to be. Apparently not good enough to get the big promotion, but I've poured all my sweat and tears into this job for years now. I can confidently say I'm proud of the work I've done and my reviews consistently show that I rarely, if ever, make mistakes with the accounts."

"Ah, so that's one of the things that sent you scurrying down here," Lucas said.

Sam leaned her head back on the seat and closed her eyes for a moment, wondering if that was how the people at work viewed her – scurrying away with her tail tucked between her legs.

"It is. I was essentially promised the CFO position. I took on every last task and challenge presented to me and worked long hours. But the guy who kissed ass and delegated the most got the job. End of story," Samantha said.

"It doesn't sound like your company rewards loyalty or hard work," Lucas said, slowing as they approached the village.

"I always thought they did. But in all honesty, now that I've had a chance to step back from it, I can see they really don't. I never received any special bonuses or vacation time that any of my other colleagues didn't receive as well. All the overtime I put in was just to claim the coveted CFO position. And for what?"

"For nothing, it seems. So, why are you giving loyalty to a company that hasn't given it to you?" Lucas asked, his tone even, though his words slammed into her like a hammer to the gut.

"Well, shit, to be honest..." Samantha said. "I have no good answer to that."

"Something to think about, I guess. Maybe there's other companies out there that would value your work more." Lucas shrugged as if he hadn't just handed her an epiphany, and slowed his truck in front of his restaurant, tapping his horn in a friendly beep. A short man, round at the waist with deep brown skin and a mile-wide smile, came out from behind the bar and over to the truck. Samantha wondered if the cars behind them would get annoyed, but it seemed people just accepted a car stopping in the middle of the road to chat. Perhaps that was the norm on the island. If this was back home, the horns would be honking madly by now.

"Hey, Javier, this is my friend Samantha," Lucas said, clasping the man's hand and pointing to Samantha, who waved to him.

"Ah, a pretty lady to join you on a pretty day," Javier said, winking at Samantha.

"Would you like to have dinner here tomorrow?" Lucas asked Samantha.

"I... yes, I would," Samantha said, still tripping over the fact that she and Lucas seemed to be actually dating.

"Save us two of your best swings, Javier. We'll

come by around seven or so," Lucas said. Javier nodded, waving at them as they motored on. Sam swiveled her head to see a line of cars behind them.

"Not a single one honked," Samantha marveled.

"Oh, the cars? No, what's the point? You're going to get mad at someone you live on a small island with? Plus, nobody is in a hurry here. Well, tourists are. You can always tell when someone is just visiting — they're always rushing around trying to pack the most into their trip." Lucas laughed. "I get it. I used to be the same way. Go, go, go."

"You're saying you learn more about life if you spend time in the slow, slow, slow." Samantha smiled as they left the colorful buildings of town behind them and headed toward the Laughing Mermaid.

"It's not a bad way to learn," Lucas said. "If you're moving too fast you might just miss what's right in front of you."

They'd pulled to a stop in front of the Laughing Mermaid, but Lucas made no move to get out as he studied her. Her mind whirled with the idea of leaving the company, of falling for this man, of living a life outside anything she'd been told was possible. Could this be the life she'd been working toward all along?

Sam wasn't used to making dramatic decisions or sudden changes, and she felt panic flutter in her chest. It was all too much at once; she needed room to breathe. Her hand moved to nervously tuck her hair behind her ear, and when she felt the comb she was immediately infused with a rush of calm. Remember the ocean, it seemed to remind her. Go with the flow.

"Thank you, Lucas, for a beautiful day," Samantha said, needing to escape and be by herself for a moment to process.

"You're welcome, Samantha. I really enjoy spending time with you and it was a delight to share some of my favorite places with you," Lucas said, his hand reaching up to twirl a lock of her hair around his finger.

"I'll never forget the turtle. I swear I almost cried right into my mask," Samantha laughed, then sobered when Lucas leaned over and kissed her softly.

"It was a special moment. The ocean shows you her love in her own way. I'm only happy that I got to experience it with you. I hope you hold onto that if you need to make any tough decisions moving forward," Lucas said, and kissed her once more.

"The ocean will be my guide?" Samantha looked up at him, his eyes seeming even more green against the fresh flush of sun on his skin.

"The ocean has loads of lessons to teach us all. You've only to listen," Lucas said, a small smile on his face. "Will you dance with me on the beach tonight, pretty mermaid?"

"Mermaid? Oh, the comb." Samantha touched it again, feeling the little hum of power it seemed to give her, and then shot him a sassy look. "I'd love to dance with you tonight."

"Good. Wear red. It drives me crazy," Lucas said. This time his kiss was decidedly dangerous as he trailed one finger down her bikini top to slip inside and cup her breast. Instantly, lust shot straight through her, and she sat there, a molten pool of need.

"Uh, I will." Samantha glared at him when he pulled back and laughed.

"Don't give me that look," Lucas said.

"You're teasing me on purpose," Samantha bit out.

"What were we just talking about?" Lucas reminded her as he got out of the truck and unloaded the picnic basket.

"Taking life slowly." Samantha sighed in frustration as she got out and stood in front of the villa.

"Exactly. And I plan to take it really nice and slow once I get my hands on you, Samantha," Lucas whispered, brushing his lips over hers once more as her cheeks flushed with heat again.

"Isn't that what siestas are for?" Samantha asked, nodding toward the second floor where her suite was. "A nice relaxing… uh, break?"

"I want you when you're ready for me," Lucas said, running his hands up and down her arms again. "Not when you're trying to rush that part because you're nervous. You and me, Sam? We're worth the wait."

Sam held onto that thought as she curled into a chair by her balcony and looked out at the water. It had been so long since anyone had put her first, or had considered her worth the wait. Even her own family hung up on the phone on her as they raced from appointment to appointment.

Maybe, for the first time, someone was valuing her for her. And wasn't that something to think about?

CHAPTER 30

"I can't wear that." Sam blanched at what looked like bluish-green fish net covered in sparkly mirrored discs, which Jolie was currently holding up in the air. "My hoo-ha will show."

"Hoo-ha?" Mirra gasped and started giggling. "How old are you again?"

"Naughty bits? Lady garden? Down there?" Samantha supplied, sending the sisters into fits of giggles as they pawed through Samantha's clothes in her room.

She'd spent her siesta time doing something she hadn't done in a really long time: thinking, with zero distractions, about her life and what she wanted from it. Ignoring her phone, her laptop, even the trashy romance novel, Sam had curled up in a shaded low-slung chair and stared out at the ocean, waiting to see what lessons it would offer her. Before long, she'd pulled out a notebook and had begun to write – not making lists or plans, just writing down all the thoughts that swirled around in her head. It was a free-form brainstorming kind of self-therapy session and by the time she was done with it, a pattern had emerged. Samantha had studied the mess of words and in one blinding moment, they'd all fit perfectly together.

She was desperately unhappy with her job. It hurt to admit that, she realized: She'd given so much of herself to her career over the years, and for what? A company that didn't treat her with loyalty or respect. But at the end of the day, if she sat back and really looked at her career, she realized she hated working for Paradiso. At first, the thought had stung, but oddly enough, after a moment, the realization had flooded her with a newfound power. It was like having a boyfriend break up with you and realizing you never loved him anyway.

The golden egg she'd been striving for all along had never been the CFO position at Paradiso. It had been the recognition of her family. And even that would have been an empty win, she realized, because it would have left her working hard for a company she hated to please people who had no idea what was best for her. They might think they did, but since they'd never bothered to really get to know her, there was no way they could know what would make her happy.

The realization had been a harsh one. Perhaps that was why she kept herself so busy all the time. If she'd stopped for a moment and truly looked around at what she was doing with her life, she'd have discovered how wildly unhappy she was. And who wants to learn that when they have no escape route? But now, Samantha mused, maybe she'd figure out a new way to live. Maybe.

Baby steps, she told herself. First things first, she needed to get her butt into a few therapy sessions when she got back home. There was some heavy stuff weighing her down that she'd need to work through. Next, she'd need to develop an exit strategy for the next year while she decided what the next stage of her life would look like. It wasn't in her to flounce dramatically from the office in a hail of curses and overturned desks. Instead, she promised herself she'd outline a new plan that would deliver the life she wanted to live, and tell nobody – well, except Lola – until she had implemented it.

By that time, hopefully she'd have had enough therapy to deal with whatever onslaught came from her family.

"Ohhh, lady garden," Jolie breathed, making Samantha jump and return her focus to the conversation. "I like that. Like you're a flower to be plucked."

"A rose yet bloomed," Mirra chuckled.

"The sweetest petals –" Jolie began, but Samantha cut her off with a screech.

"Oh my god, that's enough," Sam said, blushing as they laughed, dancing around her, a whirling circle of color and vibrant energy.

"This, darling Samantha, is meant to be worn over a skirt," Jolie laughed, holding the netting up and tying it around her flowing pink skirt. The wrap transformed the skirt into a sparkling blue-green fancy, and Samantha's eyes lit up with delight.

"Ohhh, I see. It's kind of like what belly dancers wear when they tie those chimes around their waist," Samantha said, holding her hands out. "Gimmee, gimmee."

"See? I told you she'd like it." Jolie shot a look at Mirra, who just shrugged.

"This one is nice, if a bit sedate," Mirra said, holding up a proper blue shift dress.

"He… um, Lucas, that is, said he'd like to see me wear red," Samantha said, and the sisters squealed.

"Do you have red underwear?" Jolie asked as Mirra dug into Samantha's bag of new clothes from the shop downtown.

"I have a red bra, but not matching panties," Samantha said.

Jolie waved it away. "No need for panties under a long skirt," Jolie said.

Samantha almost choked. No underwear? That seemed… entirely too decadent.

Mirra caught her look and smiled with understanding. "It's freeing, I promise."

"Baby steps, ladies," Samantha said, using her boardroom voice, and Jolie saluted in response.

"Here. This is perfect," Mirra said, dragging a dress

from the bottom of the pile, one that Sam didn't even recall purchasing. A deep siren red, it had a strapless neckline and a mermaid fit, then dropping away to the floor in a loose fringe. It was a simple dress, with blue accents embroidered at the bust and a touch of the whimsy in the fringe.

"I seriously do not remember buying this dress," Samantha said, holding it up. "It's not like anything I would ever have picked out."

"I bet it looks great on you. Charlene knows what she's doing. Go on, try it on, we'll wait," Jolie insisted, digging through Samantha's jewelry stash. Sam took the dress to the bathroom. She knew it probably made her a fuddy-duddy in their eyes, that she hadn't disrobed right there, but she'd never had sisters and wasn't used to this level of intimacy among women friends.

And wasn't it weird, she mused as she stripped, that these women had become friends so quickly? Was that the nature of island life? Or was it just the nature of these two? Because she did feel like they were her friends – or at the very least they had her best interests at heart – and she highly doubted they got this close with every guest that walked through the door.

Pulling the dress over her head, Sam quickly realized she'd have to go without a bra as well, due to the strapless neckline. No matter, though – the dress fit her like a glove and she gasped into the mirror.

Who was this woman? She'd gone from tailored suits and impeccable blouses in muted tones to wild hair, tanned skin, and a dress with a fringe that tickled her legs.

"Let's see!" Mirra called, and Samantha flung the door open, strutting out into the room.

"I told you it was perfect," Mirra exclaimed, clapping her hands.

"It's to die for," Jolie agreed, grabbing Samantha's hand and pulling her to stand in front of the full-length mirror. "Now, let's tie this on for some extra oomph."

Jolie tied the sparkly netting around Samantha's waist, transforming her dress from simple and fun to sparkly and a bit outlandish. Never in a million years would Samantha have put this outfit together.

"It looks like I'm a mermaid," Samantha laughed, turning to look at the sparkles that glittered down the back of the skirt.

"Speaking of, just the comb as the last touch," Mirra said, coming forward with the comb Lucas had found. "No more accessories needed. And go barefoot."

"Lucas found that comb in the ocean today," Samantha said, looking into Mirra's pretty blue eyes as she fussed with Sam's hair. "It looks like it's made from a shell. I wonder if the pearls are real."

"Of course they are." Mirra's eyes met hers, dead serious. "It's a mermaid comb."

"I… well, I mean, sure, it looks like one. But it's probably just from one of the village shops, right?" Samantha asked.

"No, it's a mermaid comb," Mirra said, and turned,

showing Samantha the mirror. "See? Don't you look just like a mermaid now?"

Sam could only gape at the vision she saw in the mirror. Mirra had performed some sort of intricate braid on half her hair and secured it with the comb, leaving the rest to tumble down her back in a riot of saltwater curls. Her skin looked flushed – but a healthy flush, not a nervous or embarrassed one – sunkissed, Sam decided. The dress was a bit ridiculous, loads of fun, and the sparkle wrap just added to the costume of it all.

"I suppose, if mermaids could walk, they might look a bit like this," Sam laughed. "Honestly, this is so fun! God, I don't know when the last time was that I just had fun."

"That's what we're here for. Now, channel your inner mermaid tonight with Lucas, won't you?" Jolie said, as they all piled down the steps to the main floor.

"Irma told me to do the same, but I'm not really sure what that means," Samantha said.

"It means be free with what you want in your life. Take power in your femininity. Flow with the ocean or rage if needed, but no matter what – trust in your own power," Mirra smiled, looking for all the world like a blonde angel of wisdom.

"Is that how you both seem so confident with yourselves? I'm surprised you don't have every man for miles around eating out of your hands," Samantha said, following them into the kitchen where Irma was prepping for the cookout.

"Who said they don't?" Irma asked, catching the tail end of the conversation. She let out a whistle when she saw Samantha. "And don't you look sassy this evening!"

"I can honestly say that nobody has ever referred to me as sassy before." Samantha dimpled under the compliment.

"Well, Lucas is about to get an eyeful, because once he sees you tonight, I don't think he'll be able to keep his eyes off of you."

"You think? Hmmm, I quite like that," Samantha said, sending the room into laughter.

"It's going to be a fun group tonight. A few of the neighbors and two catamarans of old friends from a neighboring island passing through."

"Is Esteben here?" Jolie demanded.

Irma nodded, sending the sisters into a frenzy. They dashed from the room without another word, and Samantha turned to look at Irma in question.

"You're not the only one who may have a hot date tonight," Irma said with satisfied smile, pouring potatoes into a pot for mashing.

"I'm sassy and have a hot date," Samantha said, testing the idea.

"No need to rub it in, dear," Irma chuckled.

CHAPTER 31

"I take it back," Samantha said to Irma hours later. "I'm not that sassy."

"Don't let my girls intimidate you," Irma laughed. "They've had years of practice owning their sensuality. You're still learning."

They watched as Jolie flitted by in a barely-there scrap of ocean blue silk that made her eyes and certain other assets pop. The sailors' eyes tracked her with hunger – well, those who weren't watching Mirra laugh her way around the fire, equally alluring in a gossamer wisp of a white lace dress.

"Doesn't it bother you?" Samantha wondered. Her own mother would never approve of the outfits these women wore, let alone how they openly flirted with various men. She'd likely call them hussies – or something worse, Samantha thought, pressing her lips together.

"That my daughters enjoy sex? No, it does not. So do I. I think it's the worst kind of slut-shaming that society does. Men are patted on the back for the number of notches they add to the bedpost, but women have to be demure and chaste their whole lives? It's just another way for the patriarchy to hold you back," Irma said. She looked resplendent in a shimmering gold dress that stopped just short of her bare feet, where one toe was adorned with a shiny toe ring. "As women of the ocean, we rise above society's standards. We're in touch with who we are, and we own our sensuality and our power. You'll learn to as well, if you spend more time here – near the water."

"I think I'd like to learn that," Samantha said. "Maybe not the notches on the bedpost thing, though it certainly sounds entertaining. But the owning my power aspect. I'd always considered myself a powerful woman in a high-level career, until I realized I haven't been making choices for me."

"See? The ocean is already working her wonders on you." Irma pressed a kiss to her cheek and gave her a gentle push toward where Lucas was walking down the sand with Pipin at his side. "Go greet your man. I've got to get the food on this BBQ."

"My man?" Samantha shook that off with a laugh, but her eyes hopped over the variety of people tucked at tables and chairs they'd pulled haphazardly onto the beach to watch the sunset. Irma had lit the large BBQ pit, and tiki torches were stuck in the sand at random points around them to ward off the bugs. Music throbbed in the background, and people had gradually wandered down the beach, joining the group with hearty welcomes. A few people already swayed to the music, and Sam found herself lost in the charm of this easy get-together where there were no rules or expectations other than to have fun. It was so far from the perfectly manicured world of seating charts and country clubs, and she wondered why she'd been striving for a life like that in the first place. This looked to be much more her speed.

Pipin raced to her, wiggling at her feet, but being a good boy and not jumping on her dress.

"Hi buddy," Samantha said, delighted that he remembered her, crouching to give him scratches that had him all but convulsing in joy.

"Go on," Lucas told the dog, "say hi to everyone." Pipin raced off in a beeline of joy to find Jolie and Mirra who instantly showered him with similar levels of affection.

"Hello," Samantha said, smiling shyly at Lucas. "You look nice." He looked more than nice, she thought, with loosely rolled green canvas pants and a white shirt that set off his tan.

"For once, I envy the enthusiasm with which my dog is greeted," Lucas murmured.

Samantha laughed. "You want me to give you belly rubs?"

"I wouldn't say no," Lucas said, stepping close to her.

Samantha glanced around to see if anyone was watching before placing a chaste kiss on his cheek. "We'll see," she laughed, then caught her breath when he pulled her close for a languid kiss for everyone to see. Samantha could feel the embarrassment creeping through her even as it was overtaken by an even stronger wave of lust.

"Just in case any of the men got any ideas about you," Lucas said, his gaze predatory as he looked at the group on the beach.

"Oh? You're claiming me?" Samantha asked, feeling a bit giddy at the thought. She'd never really had anyone be so outright… *male* about her.

"Yes," Lucas said simply, his green eyes steady on hers. The flame of a tiki torch reflected in their depths.

"I don't remember you asking," Samantha said, trying out some sass for size.

"I didn't," Lucas said, leaning over to nip at her ear, pressing a kiss to the delicate curve of her throat and sending a shiver down her body.

"What if I want to flirt with one of those men?" Samantha demanded. "We aren't dating, you know."

"Is that really what you want?" Lucas asked, his gaze steady on hers, calling her on her bullshit.

"No," Samantha sighed, "I don't."

"I'll be straightforward with you: If you're trying to make me jealous or want to play games, you should know I left that kind of nonsense back in the States."

"I couldn't play games if I tried," Samantha said,

digging her toe glumly into the sand. “I was just trying out being sassy, since Irma said my dress made me look that way.”

“It does. You’re heart-stoppingly beautiful in this dress. And you’re welcome to try out sassy as much as you want. When you’re alone. With me,” Lucas said, his eyes hot. Samantha gulped against her suddenly dry throat.

“Dinner’s on!” Irma called.

Lucas smiled, his eyes twin pools of lust.

“Saved by the dinner bell.”

CHAPTER 32

And what a dinner it was. Irma served a mixed grill, perfectly roasted over the open flame, along with sides of potatoes and salads. Everyone heaped loads on their plates, and either balanced a plate on a knee or pulled up to one of many little tables strewn across the sand. Some people laid out on blankets, laughing and talking, pointing to where the sun dropped toward the horizon.

Behind it all, the beat of the music thrummed, seeming to hum deep in her blood, and Samantha found herself wanting to dance. Not yet, of course – nobody else was dancing and it wouldn't be seemly. But maybe later she would, if other people did. Lucas had asked her to save a dance for him, so it seemed likely.

Sam eyed the rainbow-colored glass full of punch she'd been handed.

"Just how much rum is in these things?" Samantha asked.

Irma smiled as she passed by in a swirl of clinking bracelets and gold silk. "The right amount."

"Well, that tells me nothing," Samantha grumbled.

"You don't like the punch?" Lucas asked. He was making Pipin perform a ridiculous number of tricks – in her opinion, at least – before giving him a piece of hamburger.

"No, I love it. But I just feel like dancing, which is not something I usually feel like doing, so I think I'm getting tipsy," Samantha said, then sighed, reaching over to snag a bit of chicken and hand it to the patiently waiting Pipin, who devoured it in one gleeful bite. "You're torturing this poor dog."

"I am not torturing him. He knows he's not supposed to beg at the table. If he wants to beg, he will need to perform before he's rewarded with food. It's to deter him, because some people don't like dogs around the dinner table," Lucas explained patiently.

"Oh. And I just told him it was fine?" Samantha asked.

"Pretty much," Lucas grinned at her. "It's okay though. He promises to still try to be a gentleman around you."

"That seems to be theme in your household," Samantha said, a lot more harshly than she intended. Once again she eyed her rum drink.

"Is someone getting a wee bit cranky?" Lucas

laughed, and wrapped an arm around her shoulder, pulling her close so he could press a kiss to her neck.

"No," Samantha lied. "Yes. Maybe."

"Take it slow… achingly slow," Lucas whispered at her neck, sending shivers through her once more. "But first… we dance."

"Dancing?" Samantha perked up. She was a horrible dancer, and yet she loved to do it. The only time she ever got a chance to dance was at weddings, and since everyone looked like a fool at weddings, she didn't really care.

"After the sun sets." Lucas fed a patient Pipin another piece of food. "Now, watch for the green flash. It looks to be a good night for it."

"What's the green flash?" Samantha asked.

"On days where there's no clouds on the horizon – like today – as the sun slips into the sea, in the last instant before it goes beneath the horizon line it flashes a brilliant green color. I like to think it's because the sun lights the ocean with its rays and puts it to bed before the moon comes out to play."

"That's charming," Sam murmured, and snuggled into Lucas as he held her. She watched as the sun slid slowly into the ocean and, in the last instant, Sam saw it.

"The green flash!" Sam exclaimed, thinking she'd imagined it, but those around the beach were high-fiving each other and exclaiming over it.

"Cool, huh?" Mirra asked, stopping by them on her way toward the water.

"It is. Does this happen every night?"

"No, not even close. But it's a treat to see it. Just another fun thing to look forward to each day," Mirra said, and swirled on down the beach, smiling and flirting with a slew of men, leaving their jaws open as she walked past.

"I wish I could command a room like she does," Sam murmured – then realized she'd said it out loud.

"You've got a pretty strong presence too, my beauty. You just don't see it yet," Lucas said, his hand tracing circles lightly at her side.

"I'm trying," Sam said.

"Just be yourself. And have fun," Lucas said, standing up to clear their plates. He came back carrying two more rum punches, and she eyed them suspiciously.

"Those seem pretty strong," Samantha said.

"You haven't really had a vacation on an island if you don't have one night where you drink too much rum punch," Lucas teased.

"Well, then, if I must," Samantha laughed and accepted the drink. As the final rays of the sun shot into the sky, someone turned up the music and lit fire to a pile of sticks in the sand. Jolie was the first to begin dancing, confidently moving her body around the fire, dipping and swiveling, and even Samantha found herself crushing on her just a bit. Not that she was attracted to her or anything, but it was hard to look at anyone so beautiful and not have a bit of a crush.

Soon others joined, and the music got louder. With

no lights but the fire and the tiki torches and the moon up above, bodies bounced and turned, half in shadow, half in light, and flowed around the fire. Everyone was laughing, and partners swung to partners – women with women, men with men, it didn't matter. At one point, Samantha even saw Pipin on his hind legs while Mirra held his paws and shimmied with him.

"You ready to dance?" Lucas asked, tapping her now empty drink.

"Oh yeah," Samantha breathed, enamored with the carefree manner in which everyone flowed around the beach, laughing and swaying, embracing the ease of moving their bodies to the music.

Lucas pulled her close, sliding one leg between hers as the music changed to a slower, sultry song, and Samantha felt pure need course through her. Dropping her head back, she looked up at the night sky and allowed Lucas to hold her, swiveling his hips against hers as he led her in time to the beat. It seemed to swarm around her, and within – the push of the music, the heat of his body against hers – and Samantha swayed against him, swinging her hips with abandon, as they circled in the sand, completely caught up in each other. By the time the song was over, they both were dripping in a film of sweat and need. Samantha pulled back to meet his eyes and Lucas took her mouth in one punishing kiss before releasing her.

"Not yet," Lucas gasped, and spun away to dance

with a grandma who had come up and tweaked his bum with a laughing smile on her face.

Sam buried her lust down and stepped back, only to have Mirra hook her arm and twirl her into a complicated series of steps. The hours passed by in a blur of dancing – everything from hip-hop to salsa moves, and a few embarrassing attempts at a limbo that Samantha would rather not think about. She laughed until she cried, danced until she'd all but sweated through her dress, and had more fun than she'd had at any other time in her life.

Taking a break, she found her way to her bedroom to use the bathroom, then wandered back out toward the beach. Admittedly, she'd had more to drink than was usual for her, but she'd been having such a good time that she hadn't thought much of it. Now she stood in the dark on the side of the villa, and watched everyone dance around the fire – telling jokes, having fun, and belonging together. As a community.

As a family.

The sadness slammed into her so hard that she actually stumbled before she turned away and took a different path down the darkness of the beach. This was what she'd wanted all along, Samantha realized, as tears filled her eyes and spilled in streams down her face. Everything she'd been working so hard for – her job, her family, to find love – it was because she just wanted to be accepted. And the saddest part of it all? All her hard work had been for nothing.

Her co-workers weren't her family, nor were they loyal to her. She'd been too busy to make any of her relationships work, let alone make new friends or try and meet new men after her disastrous engagement. Her family only supported her if she was a good girl and played by their rules. All of it had been because her heart so desperately craved what was happening on the beach right there this night. A family of friends who accepted each other for who they were and welcomed everyone into the fold, without judgment. It didn't matter where people had come from or how they'd ended up on the island – all were welcome.

Her life – everything she'd pursued thus far – was a joke.

CHAPTER 33

Samantha walked until she found a cluster of rocks near the water where she could curl up and stare out at the water for a moment. She'd have to go back to the party soon, as she'd be missed, but she wanted to take this moment to try and process all the feelings whirling around inside her that suddenly felt too big. It was like she'd spent years keeping them locked in a vault deep inside of her.

The irony was that the one thing she'd been striving so hard for – the cushy CFO position – was exactly the key she'd needed to truly feel again, but it had been *losing* the position that was the key, not attaining it.

And, as Lola would say, ain't that a bitch?

Samantha wiped her cheeks and worked on regulating her breathing, but there was no stopping the flow of tears that poured from her. All the stress – the pain of late nights, broken relationships, frustration with her family – came pouring out as she sobbed on the rocks, wrapping her arms around her legs and staring blindly out to the dark sea.

She wanted to be Irma or Jolie or any number of the people on the beach – people who seemed so comfortable and sure of themselves. At ease with going with the flow, knowing that a friend was just a walk down the beach away. Or in Jolie's case, a man to snuggle with was a catamaran ride away. She wanted that ease… that sense of belonging.

No matter how hard she tried, she wasn't going to get it from her family. After university she'd been so busy working long hours to work her way up in the company that she'd lost the few tenuous friendships she'd had, except for Lola. She didn't just want to *be* loved, Sam realized, she wanted to give love, too. God, Lola had been right all along. What the hell was Sam working so hard for? She didn't even have awesome travel experiences to pull out and pat herself on the back for – she'd been too timid to explore foreign cities alone in the few hours she'd had free on each work trip. So here she sat, nearing forty, with no life partner, an empty shell of a condo that barely felt like a home, a career that ultimately didn't light her up inside, and an incredibly controlling family who refused to give her space to breathe and make her own mistakes. Samantha sighed. As she ran an exasperated hand through her hair, her fingers brushed the comb.

Time to buck up, Samantha ordered herself, feeling a rush of pleasure at the touch of her comb. One of the reasons she didn't typically allow herself to cry – aside from the fact she looked like a hot mess after – was that she didn't find it productive to wallow in her issues. So she forced herself to do what she always did when things got a little too achy for her to deal with.

"You've got a job a million people would die for. You get to travel. You have health insurance. A steady paycheck. Your health is good. Food on the table. An amazing best friend who is always there for your neurotic self. And your hair's not too shabby either," Samantha recited to herself. There, count your blessings and move on, she chided herself.

Still, Samantha lingered a moment more, lost in the melancholy of the moment. Counting her blessings usually helped her move past her sad moments, but tonight she was really struggling. Was it so much to want to love? The drink must be making her sappy, Sam thought.

A large flash of silver caught her eye, and Samantha caught her breath, wiping the tears away to strain her eyes in the darkness. There! Again, a flash of silver, and Sam blinked blurrily against the vision that seemed to form before her.

Was that… a woman swimming far out in the ocean? Far past where they could reach her and help her, Sam thought, surging to her feet and hoping to see it once more. When a tail, far larger than a fish, flipped above the water and the woman dipped below the sea, Sam's mouth dropped open.

"No way…" Samantha breathed.

Once more the woman surfaced, a tiny bit closer. A pulse of energy seemed to flow across the water, embracing Samantha and seeming to absorb the sadness that so ached in her soul. For a second, Samantha could have sworn the woman looked like Irma, but then she dipped once more below the waters, her tail delivering one decisive splash before disappearing from sight.

She stood, arms wrapped tightly around herself, staring wildly into the darkness of the ocean until a bark startled her away, and she turned to see Pipin racing across the sand to her.

"Hey, buddy," Samantha said, crouching to hug the delirious dog, who licked her face in delight. "You found me. Good boy."

"Samantha? What are you doing so far down here? We were worried," Lucas said, approaching slowly, his hands in his pockets. When he drew close to her, he stopped and studied her face in the pale light of the moon. "You've been crying."

Of course, it wasn't dark enough to hide what a mess she was, Samantha thought with a mental eyeroll. Then she nodded, looking away, hoping to see it – whatever it was she had seen – once again.

"What's wrong, baby?" Lucas asked, pulling her into his chest so that her arms automatically went around his waist. Despite herself, Sam immediately burst into tears again.

"I wish I could be like that," Samantha said.

Lucas waited her out, clearly not wanting to interpret her drunken logic.

"Just like the people on the beach. At ease with life. Coming together as friends and family. Knowing you've got people to rely upon. Having someone to love you just as you are. Just easy, you know? Everything in my life always feels clunky."

"Clunky?" Lucas asked, rubbing her back and gently guiding her back down the beach so she fell in step with him, his arm around her shoulder as they walked.

"Yes, clunky. Nothing flows. I have to work so damn hard for everything, and I still never get what I want."

"Which is?"

"People happy to see me," Sam whispered, feeling the tears spike her eyes again at the truth of it. "Not a burden. Not an annoying co-worker. Not an unruly daughter. Just happy to be around me."

"I'm happy when I see you," Lucas said, and Samantha felt the warmth spread through her, even though she suspected he was just being nice because he had his arms full of a weepy, tipsy woman.

"You don't really know me," Samantha said. "But that's sweet of you. I'm happy when I see you too."

"I think I see you more clearly than you see yourself," Lucas said, and Samantha realized he had steered them up the beach to the patio of his house.

"And what do you see?" Samantha whispered, looking up at his handsome face, standing so close she could see the moon mirrored in his eyes.

"I see a beautiful woman who is finally taking a long hard look at her life and realizing that she wants something different. A woman who was strong enough to walk out on a job that didn't treat her well – even if it was just for three weeks – and who is willing to take risks. I see a woman who is ready to take the training wheels off her life and ride on her own. It's a magickal thing, this point in life you find yourself at, and I'm honored to be here for it."

Could he really see all that in her? All Samantha could see was a weepy sodden mess. But his words filled her with such warmth and a sliver of excitement. Could it be that easy? Was it possible to just change her life like that? One thing was for certain, she wanted to share some of this new-found Samantha with the man who stood before her. Now.

In the bedroom.

Surprising him, Samantha launched herself at Lucas, throwing him back a few steps as she wrapped her arms around him and locked her lips to his. Groaning, he lifted her up and wrapped her legs around his waist, carrying her with one arm through his door and down the long hallway to the master bedroom. She kept kissing him, ferocious with need, as he flipped on a low light beside the massive bed.

"I want you," Samantha gasped against his mouth. "So badly. Now, it has to be now."

"Samantha," Lucas said into her mouth, pausing as she pulled her dress down in one movement, leaving it to puddle on the floor so that she stood before him, naked. The women were right about wearing no underwear, Samantha thought, sliding her hands into Lucas's hair and pulling his head down for another kiss. He backed her against the bed, lifting her so that she lay back against the pillow. A rush of dizziness hit her – from the lust, Samantha assumed – and she trailed her hand down Lucas's chest to try and unbuckle his belt. His hand stopped her.

"But…" Samantha moaned. She was getting even more dizzy.

"Sweet dreams, my mermaid. Just rest for now," Lucas said, and Samantha was surprised to see Lucas, still fully clothed, pulling the sheets over her body. Dimly she reached out for him, but he circled around the bed, coming to lie on top of the sheet next to her, still fully clothed.

"I want you," Samantha whispered, meeting his eyes. "I have such feelings for you."

"And I for you," Lucas said. "Just rest now, Sam. We'll take care of you." Lucas nodded to where Pipin had jumped on the foot of the bed and curled into a ball, putting his head on Sam's feet. She was suddenly too tired to argue, and darkness claimed her.

"She needs us, Pipin," Lucas said, and dimmed the light.

CHAPTER 34

The bright light finally annoyed Samantha enough to prop her extremely heavy eyelids open. Looking up at a ceiling that was decidedly different than her room at the guesthouse, Samantha rolled quickly to the side.

She was in Lucas's bedroom. Specifically, in his bed. Lifting the sheet and seeing that she was butt naked, Samantha let out a little squeak of dismay and pulled a pillow over her head.

Oh god, oh god, oh god, what did I do last night? Samantha racked her pounding head, trying to piece together all the rum-soaked images that flitted through her mind. Dancing, laughing… okay, that was good. Oh, nope, there was crying. Samantha sighed. She'd definitely drunk so much that she had a crying fit. Oh… and yup, she'd thrown herself at Lucas. Way to be a mature woman of the world, Samantha lectured herself as she pummeled the pillow on her face.

"Please don't smother yourself. Getting rid of a body isn't as easy as it looks on TV," Lucas said and Samantha groaned, peeking an eye out over the pillow.

Of course the man looked like a million bucks. He'd probably gotten up, gone for a run, and filled all his friends in on the crazy drunk woman still sleeping in his bed. This is why she usually stuck to wine, Samantha lectured herself. Liquor was not a good thing for her.

"Ha ha," she said, burying her face back in the pillow. A headache banged none-too-nicely against her brain and she just wanted to sneak out the back door and find her own bed and never talk to anyone ever again. Ever.

"Here, drink this," Lucas said, tapping her on the arm. Samantha pulled the pillow back down and eyed the glass of tomato juice he was holding out. In his other hand, Advil.

"Tomato juice?"

"With a few extra secret ingredients. Take this, the Advil, and go have a shower in the ridiculously expensive rain shower I had installed and you'll feel significantly better. I promise. It works for me."

Samantha sat up, clutching the sheet against her chest, still very aware that she was fully naked, and squinted at him.

"I highly doubt you often get like this," Samantha

said, accepting the glass from him and holding it up to the light.

"Didn't I tell you it wasn't an island vacation until you've had at least one night where you've had too much rum? It happens to the best of us. You can check it off your list now," Lucas said, sitting on the edge of the bed and patting her knee. Samantha took the Advil and swallowed them down, along with the surprisingly tasty drink, and handed him back the empty glass.

"Methinks you're being too kind to me," Samantha said.

"Methinks you're being too hard on yourself," Lucas parried back, then gestured with the glass toward the bathroom door. "Go, shower. I put towels and a robe in there for you. Take as long as you need." With that he strolled from the room, giving her some much-needed privacy. As soon as he was gone, Samantha scurried to the bathroom, sighing with delight when she saw that he'd even put a toothbrush out for her. The man didn't miss a trick, she thought, and stepped into the welcoming spray of the rainfall shower.

As the water slid over her shoulders, Samantha bowed her head into the spray, leaning her arms against the wall of the shower, and closed her eyes. The rhythmic pelting of the water soothed the tension in her shoulders, and she gave herself permission to let it go. Opening her eyes, she watched as the water pooled at her feet in a swirl on the pebbled stone floor and then down the drain. She imagined her embarrassment over last night following the water down the drain and out to the ocean, swimming with the…

Her head shot up.

Had she really seen a mermaid last night? The thought brought a smile to her lips. Could it really be possible? Knowing she'd probably sound like a lunatic if she told anyone – at best, it would be chalked up to an overactive imagination spurred on by too much alcohol – Samantha touched her fingers to her lips.

A secret then, just for her.

Surprisingly, the ache in her head eased as she tried out some of Lucas's minty soap and rinsed her body of the sweat and sand from a night spent dancing on the beach. When she was fully clean, Samantha toweled off, wrapping herself in the thin linen robe – which was way too big for her – and dried most of the wetness from her hair. Grateful for the toothbrush, as her teeth felt like they had a layer of sawdust on them, Samantha finished up.

"Feeling better?" Lucas asked when she stepped back into the bedroom. He was leaning against the doorframe, looking like a relaxed beach bum in a loose t-shirt and faded cargo shorts.

"So much better." Samantha smiled at him, feeling just a bit shy in his robe, but grateful for the coverage nonetheless. "Your hangover cure really works."

Lucas crossed the room and cupped her chin in his hand, lifting her face so he could study it.

"No more headaches? Stomachache? Dizziness?"

"Nope. All gone. I feel great," Samantha said.

"Good. Then we can finish what you started last night," Lucas said.

Samantha squeaked as he lifted her, depositing her firmly in the middle of his bed.

"Lucas, I'm sorry. I shouldn't have thrown myself at you like that. Not after you'd been so kind as to care for me when I was crying. It wasn't fair of me," Samantha said, trying to talk through the feelings that pulsed through her body as he nibbled gently at her neck. "I shouldn't have taken advantage of you like that."

"You can take advantage of me all you want, but I want our first time to be when you're sober," Lucas said, bracing his hands on either side of her so he could look her in the eyes. "Don't get me wrong – I don't mind a tipsy roll-around in the bed. But not for our first time. I want you to remember every moment of it."

"Um," Samantha said – very poetically, she was sure.

"'Um' is right," Lucas said, nibbling at her lips before pulling away to look her in the eye. "This matters. We matter."

CHAPTER 35

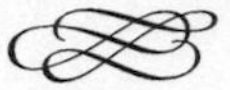

We matter, Samantha whispered to herself as Lucas took her under with his kisses. It was a simple statement, but the words wielded their power on her. When was the last time someone had put her first? Aside from Lola, nobody in her life saw her for who she was, was patient with her, or wanted to take care of her. Here was this man, whom she'd only known for a matter of days, seeing her more clearly than anyone else in her life.

Was it because she'd met him at a breaking point? When her shields were down and he could see through her tough exterior to the woman inside who begged to be loved? How could someone who'd only just met her seem to know her so well? It felt right, she realized, as she met him kiss for kiss.

Like no other man before – this felt right.

"We matter," Samantha said, aloud this time.

Lucas's smile flashed in his face and for an instant she saw the vulnerability that lay behind his confident exterior. He wanted her, but this wasn't just a game for him, she realized. He truly wanted her – all of her – and was opening himself to her.

Lucas delivered as he'd promised, exploring her with an impossible slowness that brought her body to a painfully awakened need. Tracing his lips down her jawline, he brushed his tongue lightly over the sensitive spot at her collarbone, blowing warm breath across her skin. She shivered in response, her body going liquid as she began her own exploration.

Free to touch the body she'd been staring at all week, Samantha ran her hands down the muscles of his shoulders, clenching at his back when his mouth nudged the folds of the robe aside and his mouth found her breast. Gently, he lapped at her nipple, teasing it until she panted, wanting more from him.

"Sensitive there, are you?" Lucas asked, turning his attention to her other breast until Samantha moaned beneath him, wanting him to never stop and wanting oh so much more at the same time. Her body felt loose, drugged even, and she forgot to explore more of him as he nearly brought her to the brink of pleasure simply from teasing her breasts with his mouth. By the time he moved lower, his mouth tracing a slick path over her stomach, Samantha trembled with a wet, hot need that completely undid her.

Bypassing where she wanted him most, Lucas made

his way to her feet, kneeling between her legs and smiling a wicked smile when her hands clenched the sheets. Samantha let out a little mewl of frustration.

"I still have so much to explore," Lucas said, and she jumped as he caressed her ankles, sliding his hands up to stroke gently behind her knees. It was an entirely unexpected spot to feel so damn good, and her legs trembled as he brushed a feather-light touch up and over the inside of her thighs. "Beautiful Samantha, I've wanted to unbutton you since the first day I saw you reading on the beach."

"Unbutton me?" Samantha gasped the question as he continued to gently stroke her thighs, a light rhythmic touch that had her legs opening of their own accord, all but begging for him to give her the relief she so desperately sought.

"Even from down the beach I could see how tightly wound you were. In your prim one-piece, huge beach hat, and sunglasses, and about a gazillion things to set up a wall around you. It all but said, 'go away, no touching.' It drove me crazy."

"It… I…" Samantha closed her eyes as he slid one finger across her slick heat.

"It made me want to peel back the layers, get you a little messy, see who you were without all your walls up." Lucas grinned and slid his fingers inside her in one smooth motion, and Samantha tipped over the edge and careened blissfully down the slope of the wave of pleasure that ripped through her body. Lucas continued to speak as he stroked her, bringing her right back up to the next cusp of pleasure.

"You were so much like me, you see? Wound tight, stressed to the max, and a little bit lost. I could see myself in you. No pun intended," Lucas said. Despite the onslaught he was wreaking on her body, Samantha found herself laughing helplessly as another wave of pleasure shot through her. It amazed her that she could laugh under the onslaught of sensations he was wielding on her body and his relentless attack on the walls she'd so carefully built around her heart. It had never been like this, not with any other man. The way he spoke to her, how he treasured her body, spent time teasing responses out of her so he could learn what she liked – no man had taken this much time with her before. None of them had truly wanted to.

"Don't you see?" Lucas asked, pulling away and kissing his way back up her body. She felt the hard length of him press against where she wanted him most, and she moaned, wrapping her legs around his back to bring him closer. "My soul recognized yours."

Totally lost in his words and the emotions he was pulling from her, Samantha all but drowned in the tawny green depths of his eyes as he drove into her, claiming her as his. A part of this scared her: He wasn't allowing her to hide her deepest self from him in a cloud of alcohol or a quick vacation hookup – he was speaking to her heart. Lost on the tidal wave that rolled over her,

Samantha hung on as Lucas showed her what love could really feel like.

And when they both finished, trembling together in one final rush of pleasure, Samantha clung to him and wondered if she would ever be the same.

CHAPTER 36

"I should go back," Samantha said, later in the day. They'd made love two more times and she felt weak and wobbly – and if she had to admit it to herself, more than a little vulnerable.

"Okay. Don't forget our date tonight," Lucas said, brushing a hand down her arm and pulling at a lock of her hair.

"Date?" Samantha asked, shivering in response to his touch.

"Yes, date. Remember? You said you wanted to eat dinner while you sat in a swing at my restaurant. The lady asks and I shall deliver."

"Oh, I completely forgot," Samantha said and then blushed. Was it rude that she'd forgotten he'd asked her for dinner?

"I'll take that as a compliment to my lovemaking," Lucas said, teasing her before he leaned in for a long, hungry kiss. When she pulled back, his eyes had that lusty look about them that she was already beginning to know too well.

"Save it for later. After dinner. Maybe we'll even have a tipsy roll in bed after dinner," Samantha said with a laugh.

Lucas kissed her hand. "Wouldn't that be fun? I'll get you to show me your secrets."

"I think you've seen most of them."

"I'll find more. So much to discover…" Lucas called after her as she laughed her way down the walk and crossed the beach. It was another stunning day in paradise, Samantha mused, a smile hovering on her lips as she took in the turquoise water lapping at the sand. A light breeze tickled her hair. It wasn't hard to see the appeal of living someplace like this. Even though Lucas had stressed that island life had its own unique set of challenges, the views more than made up for it, in her opinion.

Samantha hummed her way up the path to the Laughing Mermaid, then let out a little shriek as Jolie popped out seemingly from nowhere to accost her.

"Aha! The walk of shame," Jolie said, hand on hip as she eyed Samantha's dress – the same one she'd worn last night.

"Ah…" Samantha was about to make up a lie, then realized she had nothing to feel guilty about. "Damn right. And if I recall, that's exactly the same outfit you had on last night too."

"No shame here," Jolie said, flouncing hair that was decidedly messier than it had been the night before. "And I'd call this more of a strut than a walk, no?"

Jolie swaggered up to the house, a giggling Samantha in tow. At the base of the stairs, she turned and grabbed Samantha's shoulder, surveying her with a surprisingly serious look.

"Did he take care with you?"

"He did. I made a fool of myself last night and he was a total gentleman," Samantha said.

"Good. Now, I consider you a friend, so don't take this wrong the way – but if you hurt him, I'll hunt you down and make you sorry. Understood?"

"Me? Hurt him?" Samantha's mouth dropped open. She was so used to everyone running roughshod over her and her feelings, it had never once occurred to her that she could have the power to hurt him. It felt odd to have the tables turned on her.

"He's a good man. Take care with his heart," Jolie said, and squeezed her arm before disappearing into a door down the hallway. Musing over her words, Samantha peeled off her clothes and snuggled into her own bed, more than ready for a siesta after the unexpectedly athletic morning she'd had.

Even so, she found herself giggling and pounding her feet against the bed. For once, she was deliriously happy. She couldn't even bring herself to tell Lola about the newest developments yet. Somehow it had gone from something innocuous and fun to gossip about to meaning so much more. Samantha wasn't ready for it to be picked apart, or even to gush over it with anyone. She wanted this pure moment of bliss all to herself for now.

It was a feeling she didn't want to forget when reality claimed her at the end of her vacation.

CHAPTER 37

"She saw me, you know," Irma told Lucas. He'd been lounging in his hammock, idly throwing the ball for a happy Pipin when Irma had strolled up to chat.

"You showed yourself to her? I'm surprised," Lucas said, studying her. He still remembered the first time he'd seen Irma in her true form. It had taken many a night of rum and more than one discussion with the ladies before he'd finally believed that there was more than met the eye with his neighbors. Only when he'd learned that they had shown themselves to him because they truly trusted him had Lucas accepted the gift of both their power and the vulnerability they'd given to him. He'd never told a soul.

Granted, he was always honest when he told people he believed in mermaids. Typically they laughed it off and it ended with that. But the hard, honest truth was that he was living on an island where mermaids existed. He'd never wanted to give them a reason to distrust him. As a result, they'd taken him into the fold like he was family and he'd enjoyed more than one night watching them frolic through the waves, while he smiled from the beach in amazement that such magick existed in this world.

"I'm not sure she'll remember. The rum hit her fairly hard. But she needed to see – to believe in something more than her sorrow in that moment." Irma shrugged, looking out to the ocean she called home.

"She was having a moment." Lucas wasn't sure he felt comfortable sharing Samantha's woes with Irma either.

"I see a lot of you in her," Irma said. Lucas's lips quirked involuntarily as he thought about his rude joke earlier that day, but luckily Irma was still looking out to the waves. "She craves family."

"I may have been lost when I came here, but I still had a support system," Lucas said. "I feel like Samantha's broken."

"There's nothing wrong with getting broken. That's how the light gets in to push out the darkness," Irma said, turning to smile at him. "And I think it's your job to help her trust in others again."

"That's a big job to take on," Lucas said. "I can't heal other people. I could barely get myself together, if you remember."

"You're stronger than you realize. So is she. Sometimes all somebody needs is someone who has faith in them. You can build a foundation with this one, Lucas. I like her for you," Irma said, crossing her arms over the tie-dye sarong she'd wrapped around herself.

"I like her for me too. But let's be honest – it's early days yet. She still plans to go home. Where does that leave me?"

"That's what you'll have to figure out," Irma said.

"It seems like a lot to expect of someone – to ask them to give you a chance when they've only just met you," Lucas pointed out, bending dangerously low out of the hammock to scoop up the ball Pipin had dropped in the sand.

"The heart knows." Irma tapped her chest.

"Does it, though? That could be good old-fashioned lust, you know," Lucas said.

Irma laughed, shaking her head at him. "You're old enough to know the difference."

"We still have so much to learn about each other. What if it all goes wrong?"

"Ah, humans. You waste so much time waiting for everything to be perfect. Don't you understand that there is no perfect? Being alive is the perfect. That's it. Be alive together and embrace the moment. You'll figure out each other's quirks and what makes the other person furious or cry or laugh. But this…" Irma touched her chest once more. "This knows."

"I can't argue with you when you play the human

card," Lucas grumbled, and Irma bent to tousle his hair and give him a kiss on the cheek.

"I wanted you for one of my daughters," she said, "Hell, I even sized you up for myself once upon a time. You know we take so much pleasure in the more sensual aspects of living."

"Ah…" Lucas felt tongue-tied for the first time in a long time.

"But I knew you weren't for us. I wondered why, but I trusted that. I think Samantha is the why. She's here, Lucas," Irma said. Then, having dropped a decidedly worrisome bomb in the middle of the otherwise relaxing siesta he'd been having, she strolled away.

That's what women did, he thought, glowering down at Pipin. They came in and messed up an existence that he was currently enjoying quite a bit. He answered to no one and lived his life as he pleased. And as far as he could tell, life with Samantha would be a rollercoaster of emotions; the woman was not remotely easygoing – laughing one moment and stammering or crying the next. And if he was honest with himself, he was lonely. Lucas saw a deep vulnerability beneath Samantha's steel spine. A wounded flower, Lucas thought, and threw the ball for Pipin again.

He only needed to help her find her roots so she could finally bloom.

CHAPTER 38

"I'm so excited to try your restaurant," Samantha exclaimed while Lucas found a parking spot later that evening. She'd been right – there really weren't many marked parking spots. Cars were tucked haphazardly where there was space along the side of the road and in alleys, and nobody seemed to pay any mind.

"It's nothing fancy, but I hope you'll like it," Lucas said, casually reaching for her hand. Samantha felt a delightful little tingle trail up her arm. This was nice, strolling the little village where people greeted Lucas by name and music carried out of the open-air bars and restaurants. It was so different than back home, where everything was closed up and air-conditioned. Here the restaurants were open to the ocean breezes that carried the spicy scents of the fresh catch or the nightly special.

"I don't need fancy," Sam said. "I wanted to go there because it looked fun."

"You haven't had a lot of fun in your life, have you?" Lucas asked as they drew near his restaurant.

"Unfortunately, not really. You'll have to teach me," Samantha said with a laugh, and smiled as Javier hailed them from behind the bar. The restaurant was doing a brisk business and Samantha could see why. It was built around a few large palm trees, which poked up through the roof, and twinkle lights were hung in streams across the ceiling. Low music pulsed through the restaurant and nearly all the swings hanging at the long teak bar were taken. Two swings, tucked around the corner of the bar, had a reserved sign in front of them.

"Those would be ours. Best seats in the house," Lucas said, nodding at people as he tugged her to the corner and gave Javier a complicated handshake over the bar.

"These are great," Samantha said, and hoisted herself onto one. She'd worn loose palazzo pants that evening, on account of the swing, and a breezy pink blouse with hibiscus flowers scattered across it. The swings were suspended on thick nautical-style rope, and rocked easily when Samantha gave a gentle push against the bar with her feet. Delighted to find her feet didn't touch the ground, Samantha laughed, gleefully swinging back and forth a bit.

"You like?"

"It's so ridiculous and so simple," Samantha laughed

at him as he sat next to her, "but it just brings back this feeling of childhood. What a great idea."

"Thanks. I wanted to do something just a little different. We've had a really good response to it," Lucas said.

"I can imagine," Sam said. "Plus look at this view. You can look out over the water during the day and at night still watch people stroll through town. If the food is any good, I'd say you've got a winner on hand."

"We kept the food pretty simple. We offer some local dishes and bar food, just a good mix of easy food so almost anyone can find something to eat. Is there anything in particular you're craving?" Lucas asked.

Sam knew he wasn't implying anything with his question, but she couldn't help but eye him hungrily. Catching her meaning, he laughed and leaned over to brush a soft kiss on her lips.

"That would be for dessert," Lucas said.

"Oh," Samantha breathed, and then was relieved to be distracted by a beaming Javier.

"Something to drink for the pretty lady?"

"Just a red wine, please. A Malbec if you have it," Samantha said, not wanting a repeat of last night.

"Same for me, Javier," Lucas nodded and then looked at her. "The special is usually the best on the menu – do you have anything you prefer not to eat?"

"No," Samantha said, sliding a glance over the menu. "I travel too much to be picky about food."

"Perfect. I'll just order us two specials then." Javier

nodded as he poured them two glasses of wine, then pointed to a man and a woman who had just walked in.

"From the new eco-resort. They wanted to speak with you about perhaps doing some catering and the like," Javier said.

"That's for you to decide." Lucas nodded at the couple, who were already making their way over.

"They also wanted to talk to you regarding some of your consulting services. Plus, they're new on the island. I think they're just trying to make friends. Make nice," Javier ordered, and winked at Samantha.

"When am I not nice?" Lucas wondered.

Samantha laughed. "I'm sure you have your moments. Weren't you the one telling me you were happy to move further away from town because it meant fewer people for you to deal with?"

"Fine, fine. I have my moments," Lucas grumbled. "But I'm on a date here."

"I don't mind. Really. Have a quick chat with them and we'll have plenty of time to continue our date after."

Lisa and Ben turned out to be a married couple who had invested heavily in their dream of building up an ecologically friendly tourist footprint on the island. Soon, Ben had drawn Lucas deep into a conversation about potential portfolio investments and Lisa turned to Samantha.

"I'm so sorry, I can see we're interrupting your date. I'll let Ben chatter on for a few more minutes and then drag him away. I don't want to be rude," Lisa said. A tall woman, with intelligent blue eyes in a kind face, she kept her hair short and her attire simple. Samantha liked her immediately.

"It's no bother, really. How long have you been living here?" Samantha asked.

"We moved here three years ago from California. We own the Eco-Villas along the water. Naturally, the build-out has taken longer than expected, as does everything on an island, but I'm happy to be close to finishing the last section of our properties."

"Are you booking any out at the moment?"

"Yes, we've been booking our finished ones for almost a year now. Unfortunately, we ran into a huge problem with our finance guy." Lisa sighed and shook her head, lifting one hand to wave it away. "We still need to figure out what we're going to do, as he cost us quite a bit of money. But once again, that seems to be the way of things on the island. One stumbling block after another. I am learning to practice patience and roll with it all."

"Let me guess – someone was skimming the books?" Samantha asked. She'd seen it time and again in her work, especially in foreign countries where money flowed easily and reports to the IRS were often fudged.

"Among other things." Lisa's lips tightened and Samantha could read the distress in her eyes. "It's caused a lot of sleepless nights. We'll get through it, but we haven't found anyone else we trust with our books yet. And neither of us are fully qualified in that department. So, yeah, my stress level is higher than I'd like it to be, living in paradise."

"How are your bookings?" Samantha asked, wondering if there was any demand.

"We're swamped. There's a huge demand. I feel like there's so much to manage between finishing the build-out, getting reliable staff in, making sure guests have an excellent experience… So it's just been a huge blow." Lisa laughed a bit and shrugged, saying, "Enough about us. You don't need to hear our tales of woe while on a date. Do you live here?"

"No, I'm just here on holiday," Samantha said.

"That's lovely. Have you been able to explore the island?"

"Yes, Lucas is an excellent guide. He showed me your places the other day. You've really got a beautiful spot for your rentals. I suspect customer acquisition costs will be low and retention rate high." Samantha said.

Lisa's gaze sharpened. "What do you do for work back in the States?" she asked.

"Actually, I'm an accountant for the Paradiso Hotels Luxury Portfolio," Samantha said. "So when I say I'm sorry to hear about your finance guy – I really am. It's people like him who give us a bad name."

"Lisa, let's go. These two are on a date," Ben said, coming over to smile sheepishly at Samantha. "I'm sorry, I didn't realize you were just here visiting. Enjoy your time together. We can catch up with Lucas when she's gone."

Samantha felt a weird little twinge in her stomach when Ben spoke of her departure. She wasn't ready to leave this place just yet.

"At the risk of being too forward," Lisa said, pulling a card from her purse and handing it to Samantha, "if you ever think about moving here, we could use someone like you."

"I…" Samantha said, completely taken aback.

"Just think about it. Perhaps you could take a moment to meet with me before you go – see the property and take a look at the books." Lisa shot a smile at Ben, who was now dragging her away. "Enjoy your date. This place has the best food."

"They were nice," Lucas said, while Samantha's mind whirled with possibilities.

"They were," Samantha agreed. She started to say more, wanted to ask what it would be like if she didn't go home, but then stopped herself. That was too much to put on this man. She'd only known him for a few days. It would be impossible to expect him to change his entire life for her.

But could she change hers for him? Or maybe not even for him – she could come here and rent out long term at the Laughing Mermaid until she found her own little place. Even if things didn't work out with Lucas, maybe she'd still find her spot here.

Then the thoughts were pushed to the back of her head as Javier arrived with a steaming platter of food. Samantha almost spilled her wine on herself as she bounced in her swing in delight.

For right now, she was going to savor the moment.

CHAPTER 39

Her time on Siren Island flew by in a blur of laughter, intense pleasure, and new discoveries. Samantha's senses felt heightened, as if she laughed a little louder, colors were brighter, and even food tasted better.

Or maybe that was what love did to you.

Samantha wrapped her arms around herself in a little hug of delight. She and Lucas hadn't said the words yet; frankly, when had there been the time? They'd been so engrossed in each other and exploring the island together that she'd barely thought about even checking her phone.

She had to now, though. Her flight left tomorrow night; at the very least, Samantha had to check and see if it was still scheduled for the same time. She'd even been ignoring Lola's increasingly frantic text messages, though Sam knew she'd need to respond soon.

It just felt like she was in a bubble of happiness, and if she exposed it to anyone on the outside world, they'd pop it.

Unfortunately, Lucas had client meetings today that he couldn't reschedule, which left Samantha to her own devices. After scheduling a short meeting of her own, Samantha decided to end her time on the island where she'd started it – with the romance novel on the beach. She'd never gotten around to finishing the book, as she'd spent too much time living her very own romance novel to bother. Now, picking it up, she was proud of herself for not even being embarrassed by the couple writhing on the cover. Stretching out in the red bikini she'd come to love, Samantha lost herself in the book, pushing reality away for just a bit longer.

Until her phone pinged. And pinged several more times. She shouldn't have brought it down here, Samantha thought, putting the book aside, but she'd wanted to snap a few pictures for Lola. The last time she'd had the phone down here, there had been no reception. But it must have been a fluke, for now a flood of messages demanded her attention. Sighing, Samantha picked up her phone and scanned them.

Your father and I would like to know what is going on with you. You don't answer our messages, you don't email. Have you lost your mind? When are you getting back to work?

Samantha pressed her lips together as the same bitterness she always felt at their overbearing attitude washed through her. Why couldn't they ask how she was doing or whether she was having fun? Instead, they presumed something had to be wrong with her because she hadn't jumped on a plane and flown home like they'd demanded.

If you recall, the last time you spoke with me was to tell me to have a nice life. Samantha typed back.

That's just your father spouting off. You know how he is. What we want to know is what's wrong with you? Something is obviously going on.

It hurt, Samantha realized, more than she wanted it to. It hurt that her mother could so casually dismiss how mean her father could be and immediately go back to assuming that something was wrong with her daughter. Before she could shoot off an angry reply, Irma appeared and dropped into the chaise lounge next to her.

"What's wrong?" Irma asked, cutting right to the chase.

"Is it that obvious?" Samantha asked.

"You look tense again. Like you did when you first came. Something had to have happened to put that look on your face," Irma said, stretching out on the lounge.

"It's my family – my parents specifically. Just more text messages wanting to know what's wrong with me, when will I get back to my job and work harder for the next promotion, that kind of thing." Samantha shrugged. "The last time we spoke my father told me to have a nice life, and now, weeks later I'm getting messages asking why they haven't heard from me? Um, really?"

"I'm sure that must be hurtful," Irma said, her voice full of concern.

"It's mean. And then it messes with my head and makes me think that I'm doing something wrong, when I'm absolutely not doing anything wrong other than having a vacation and dating someone I adore. Which, by the way, at thirty-eight years old is completely and totally normal to do."

"Have you told them about Lucas yet?"

"Remember the 'have a nice life' comment? I haven't heard from them since. But I'm the bad one for not reaching out to them? Anyway, there wasn't exactly an opportune time to tell them I've met someone."

"Plus, you're not really required to tell your parents about all the hot times you're having with the hunky neighbor next to the B&B you're at."

"Exactly!" Samantha said, stabbing a finger in the air. "I get to date who I want."

"What are you looking for from them, Sam?" Irma asked, turning to hold Samantha's hand. "Really and truly?"

"I want them to just love me for who I truly am. I want to be able to tell them about the things I'm doing and have them say how wonderful it is, instead of telling me what I should be doing or what's wrong with what I'm currently doing. They always lead with their opinion first and never sit back to just listen to me. It's like they have this version of me in their mind and that's what they're sticking to."

"Do you think you can change them?" Irma asked.

"No," Samantha said, and squeezed Irma's hand.

"Why haven't you changed your expectations of them? Perhaps there's a way to reframe your relationship that you don't continue to get hurt by expecting something different of their actions each time, and they can still feel like they're involved in your life," Irma suggested.

"How do I do that?" Samantha asked.

"A day at a time," Irma smiled. "Remember, your parents are human too. Everyone has faults. It's likely they love you in the only way they've been taught or know how to. It's your job to not let that get in the way of the person you're meant to be."

Samantha blew out a long breath. As if she didn't already have enough heavy thoughts on her mind, knowing she'd have to leave Lucas and this place, which had become something of a sanctuary, tomorrow.

"Everything's good, Mom. Thanks for checking on me. I love you." Samantha read it out loud as she typed it, then hit send.

"There," Irma said, smiling at her. "Doesn't that feel good?"

Samantha waited for a response, but none came.

"See? She can't even say 'I love you' back."

"Just because she can't say it doesn't mean she doesn't feel it. You can protect yourself and keep your boundaries up, but still give them love," Irma said.

"That's going to be a strong learning curve. I feel

like I keep trying to show them the real me and then getting rejected. They want to see a different version of me."

"Then go where you're wanted," Irma said.

Samantha tilted her head at her in question. "What's that mean?"

"You have people in your life who love you and see you for who you are. Why are you standing on stage begging for applause from the audience when the people who are clapping for you are in your dressing room?"

"Um…" Samantha had no good answer for that.

"Exactly. Now, spend a little time reflecting in this beautiful space. Or read that naughty book you brought with you. Either way, be at peace, pretty one. We'll see you for dinner tonight," Irma said, pressing a kiss to her cheek and strolling away.

She hadn't said a word about Lucas, Samantha realized.

Or maybe she'd said her piece.

CHAPTER 40

"Are you sure you want to come home?" Lola asked as Samantha was getting ready for the little going-away dinner they were having on the beach that night.

"No, I don't. But as much as I'd love to stay here forever, this isn't reality," Samantha said, annoyed at everything. She'd already tried on all her dresses and tossed them all in a heap on the bed. Fuming, she sat on the side of the mattress and stared out the window to where the sun was lowering toward the horizon.

"Why can't it be?"

"Because you can't just live in a hotel and have vacation sex for the rest of your life," Samantha grumbled, picking at a loose bead on one of her dresses.

"Well, no, you can't just live in a hotel the rest of your life – unless you're one of those fancy New York women that just, like, live in hotels. Could you imagine?

Anytime you're hungry you just ring for room service. Shopping? Oh, bring the car around. I mean, it's mad. That lifestyle is so beyond," Lola chattered.

"I know," Samantha said, plopping her chin into her hand.

"But, that aside, you could rent an apartment down there, couldn't you? You said there's loads of rental properties on the island. And residency doesn't seem to be a problem. If you love it there so much, why don't you try?"

"And do what? Just leave my job at Paradiso? Pack up my apartment into boxes? Make Lucas think I'm crazy because I'm dropping everything to be with him? You know what they called that in… what was that movie? *Wedding Crashers*?"

"Yes," Lola sighed, knowing where she was going with this one.

"A stage-five clinger. That's what I would be if I rearranged my entire life to show up on this man's doorstep after only knowing him three weeks."

"He sounds different than the others you've had, Sam. I think you can trust this guy," Lola said, her voice soft.

"I do trust him. But it's too soon. I can't make these kinds of decisions in a bubble of vacation sex and non-reality. What happens if I move here and he figures out just how neurotic I am? And needy? And weird?" Samantha demanded.

"It doesn't take three weeks of vacation sex to figure

that out about you," Lola said, and laughed when Samantha growled into the phone. "I'm just saying… this guy can see you for who you are. And he's still right there. Blowing your mind with great sex and taking you on new adventures each day. Why not give it a chance?"

"Well, I'm not saying no. I'm just saying, does it have to be so absolute? You know I'm total shit at making huge decisions. Can't we just, like, date long distance a bit and see how we do?"

"Is that what you want?"

"I don't know what I want! I don't want to leave him and I have to, that's all I know," Samantha said.

"Listen, I can't make this choice for you. But I will say this, Samantha – I love you and I'm here for you. I will always support you, no matter what you do. Also, I'm kick-ass at packing and selling things and I have a key to your condo, an excellent shipping company, and extra storage in my basement. So, the offer stands – I will do this for you if you promise me one thing."

"What's that?"

"Well, two things. First, a place to stay in paradise if you do end up living there."

"Done," Samantha said on a weak laugh.

"And two – for once, don't let your head get in the way of what your heart wants. Every time in your life that you've followed what other people have wanted for you, you've ended up unhappy. Just once, maybe take a chance on yourself."

"I don't know if I'm strong enough to do that."

Samantha could feel the panic racing through her at the thought of quitting her very stable job and all the stock options, health benefits, and career advancement she would lose out on.

"I know you are. It's just a matter of whether you're ready to see what I see."

"I love you, Lola," Samantha said.

"I love you, too, Sam. I expect a phone call tomorrow – no matter what you decide. I'm here for you."

"Promise."

Samantha hung up, more torn than ever. She had more options than she'd told Lola about, but she wasn't ready to voice them. First she needed to speak with Lucas.

At the knock on her door, she jumped up.

"I'll be down in ten."

"Hurry up," Jolie called through the door. "The sun's about to set."

Grabbing one of the red dresses she'd bought from Charlene the first day she'd stumbled into the village, Samantha tugged it over her head, then picked up her now-favorite comb to tuck among her curls. Just touching it seemed to give her power, and she smiled at the woman she saw standing in the mirror.

"I like you," Samantha said to her reflection.

CHAPTER 41

"Surprise!"

The quiet dinner Samantha had been expecting was anything but. They'd thrown together another beach BBQ, much like the one she'd had so much fun at, and invited all the neighbors down the beach, whom she'd come to know by name over her time here. Javier waved to her from where he manned the grill, Irma hovering close by to offer her input. Jolie and Mirra came forward, each of them grabbing her in a hug-sandwich, and Samantha clung to them.

"I'm going to miss you two so much," Samantha exclaimed.

"All the more reason to come visit often," Mirra smiled.

"A gift, for you," Jolie said, and held out a brightly wrapped box.

"You didn't have to get me anything," Samantha

gushed. "It should be me getting you gifts. You've done so much to make my time here special."

"You're more than just a guest," Jolie said with a shrug, and then narrowed her eyes. "Open it."

"Yes, ma'am," Samantha said, laughing as she blinked back a sheen of tears. Opening the box, she found a long delicately braided silver chain with a mermaid pendant on it. The mermaid's tail looped around a perfect pearl, which looked just like a full moon.

"It's stunning," Samantha breathed.

"We at the Laughing Mermaid think you've got a lot of potential," Mirra said. It took Sam a minute to realize she was quoting a line from *Pretty Woman*.

"Aww, you think I can really be a mermaid someday?" Samantha laughed and put the necklace on, loving the feel of it against her chest.

"I think you've done a damn good job of learning how to channel your inner mermaid," Irma said, coming to stand by them and pulling Samantha in for a hug. "You've come a long way in a short time. You're leaving here a different woman than the one who arrived stressed out and broken down."

"I feel different," Sam said, hugging her back.

"Good. I hope you take that feeling home with you," Irma said, then pulled back to give her a stern look. "No tears, Missy. We'll see you again soon – soon enough."

"You think?" Samantha asked.

"If you will it, so shall it be," Irma said and turned

her to see Lucas waiting on the edge of the circle, Pipin at his feet. "Now go hug that man and make a wish on the green flash."

"How do you know there'll be a green flash tonight?"

"The best nights always have them," Irma said.

Samantha crossed the sand, going as neatly and naturally into Lucas's arms as if she'd always done so. When a cold nose nudged her knee, she realized her mistake.

"I'm sorry, Pipin," Samantha said, throwing Lucas an apologetic look before crouching to give Pipin all the love he was due. Once he was satisfied, he wandered away to collect his accolades from the rest of the attendees.

"Hey," Lucas said, dropping a kiss on her forehead as he pulled her in for a snuggle.

"Hey," Samantha replied, loving the feel of him in her arms. It was as though she'd finally found home. They stood in silence, holding on to each other, as the sun dipped below the horizon. And in the last instant, Samantha saw the flash of green.

She closed her eyes and wished.

"I missed you today," Lucas said, pulling back to look down at her. "I thought about you all day long."

"I know, I missed you too. I… it's tough to think about tomorrow," Samantha said.

Just then the call for food went up.

"You get two hours. Then I'm stealing you from the

party so we can have our own private time," Lucas said, his eyes serious.

Samantha nodded. "I promise not to drink the rum," she said, and Lucas smiled.

"Best not. I want you clearheaded for what I have in mind."

Samantha gulped, but couldn't keep the smile from her face. She wanted this, she realized, so badly. Neighbors who came by for a drink, people who waved to her on the street, a chunky dog who wanted nothing more than snuggles each day… and him.

But he hadn't said he loved her, or that he wanted her to stay.

Remember, Samantha chided herself, island life is all about taking it slow. You don't need to decide your entire future in a day. The thought helped soothe the panicky feeling that clawed at her chest. She'd always been horrible at making important decisions quickly.

"I got you a little bit of everything," Lucas said, coming back with two plates in hand and a smile for her on his face.

"That's exactly what I wanted," Samantha said and pushed all thoughts of tomorrow aside to give herself over to the flow of the evening.

And as they danced – Samantha jumping up this time as soon as the music started, comfortable now in her skin – the full moon rose over them, blessing them all with its abundance and light.

CHAPTER 42

True to his word, Lucas snuck her out of the party exactly two hours later, a happy Pipin on their heels. Instead of steering her toward his villa as she had expected, he tugged her down the beach.

"Let's walk in the moonlight. It's so pretty tonight, no?"

"It really is," Samantha said, happy just to be near him. It was amazing how bright the light of a full moon could be when there was so little ambient light from a big city to compete with it. She could easily see where to place her feet, and watch as little crabs scuttled out of the way on the sand. "It's just so beautiful here."

"Are you going to miss it?" Lucas asked, his hand tight on hers.

"Of course I'll miss it. It'd be hard not to miss paradise," Samantha said, her tone light though her heart screamed that he was the one she'd really miss.

"What about me? Will you miss me?" Lucas asked, pausing to pull her toward him so he could wrap his arms around her.

"Yes, I'll miss you," Samantha said, smiling shyly up at him.

"I'll miss you, too," Lucas said, leaning to kiss her.

Samantha lost herself in him, in the moment, wanting to burn it into her brain forever.

"I… maybe I can come back and visit soon?" she ventured, anxiety clawing at her throat.

"I don't want you to visit," Lucas said, slamming the door on her hope quite neatly.

"Oh… I guess I misread this," Samantha said, stepping back from him.

"No… that's not what I meant, damn it," Lucas said, raking his hand through her hair. "Samantha, I don't want you to just come back and visit."

"I know, I know. You've said," Samantha said, turning to look back out at the water. She would not cry, she promised herself. She'd cried enough on this vacation.

"I'm asking you to stay," Lucas said, grabbing her shoulder to turn her back to him.

"You want me to stay?" Samantha said, in surprise.

"Yes, I want you to stay. I want you here, with me. Laughing in the water when we snorkel, scolding Pipin when he steals food, waking up in my bed. I want you here with me."

"But… I don't know what that means," Samantha said. "We've only just met. My life back home…"

"Screw your life back home," Lucas bit out, sounding seriously angry for the first time since she'd met him. "You're not happy there. Your work doesn't value you. Your family doesn't respect you. Stay here. With me."

"Lucas… I mean, I can certainly look at extending my vacation time. I'm more than due the time off." Samantha bit at her lip, feeling anxiety claw its way through her stomach. How was she supposed to make such a huge decision at the snap of her fingers? After she'd only known this man for three weeks? It went against everything she knew about herself – everything she was. And yet she'd been in tears over the thought of leaving him just hours before. Her head was conflicting with her heart, and panic set in.

"I don't want you to just extend your vacation time, Samantha. I want you to stay here. With me. To give us a chance," Lucas said, his eyes liquid in the light of the moon.

"But that's not fair. I have to give up everything to give us a chance? It's all or nothing? What about long distance? Can't we meet in the middle?" Samantha cried, her mind trying to look for ways they could make this work that didn't entail her throwing her entire existence as she knew it out the window.

"Long distance won't work for someone like you," Lucas said. "You need too much reassurance."

"So you're saying I'm needy?" Samantha said, stung by his words.

"No, I'm saying that you don't trust easily. And you have every right to feel that way after what you've been through. But I can't give you what you need unless you're with me."

"If you know me at all, you have to know you're asking me to make a huge life decision on… on nothing. Weeks of knowing someone!" Samantha exclaimed, and now it was Lucas who drew back, stung.

"I didn't realize I was 'nothing' to you, Samantha. I thought we had something deeper than that," Lucas said, stepping further back from her. Samantha suddenly felt like she was sinking in quicksand and couldn't get out.

"We do, it's just… I can't think straight. I'm scared and nervous and don't know what to do," Samantha said, holding her hands up in the air. "What do you want from me?"

"To make a decision that puts you first," Lucas said quietly. Turning, he whistled for Pipin and walked away. "I'll leave you to think about it."

"Oh – you say I don't trust easily and yet you walk away at the slightest argument?" Samantha yelled after him.

"I may be walking away, but you're the one leaving," Lucas said, shaking his head sadly as he disappeared over a dune toward his house.

"This is complete shit," Samantha bit out, turning to stare out at the sea. "The man wants me to just up and leave everything? To trust in him? What about my life? How am I supposed to believe in him?"

"Maybe you need to believe in yourself."

Samantha whirled to find nobody behind her. Was she hallucinating now? Was this the breaking point everyone had told her was coming when she had not gotten her promotion? Or what if this entire vacation was one big hallucination? One messed-up long dream that she hadn't woken up from yet? Samantha felt a hysterical giggle stick in her throat – then a flash of silver out in the sea caught her eye.

"Oh no you don't, not this time," Samantha raged. Irrationally she stormed into the dark water, determined once and for all to get to the heart of the matter.

CHAPTER 43

Samantha dove into the dark water, so enraged at everything that she didn't even consider what she was doing. She began to swim. The path of the full moon lit her way as she paced herself, swimming toward where she'd last seen the silver flash. Salt water filled her eyes – or were they tears? – and as the reality of what she was doing hit her, she began to tremble.

Why was she swimming out into the dark ocean after a fantasy? What did she hope to find out here?

Why had she even come here at all?

Tears streaked down Samantha's face as she began to lose steam. Her limbs began to feel heavy as the rage seeped away, to be replaced by sadness, until she felt like she could just slip under the water.

A flash of silver caused her to twist in the water. Then another flash and a splash, and Samantha twisted again.

"Don't give up, Samantha," Jolie said from over her shoulder and Samantha opened her mouth to scream, only to suck in a huge mouthful of seawater. Sputtering, she sank below the surface – but not before she saw what she'd come out here to see.

Mirra and Jolie, both heartachingly beautiful, circled her as mermaids. Their hair twined in the water, flowing behind them in waves, and their tails, shining effervescent in the light, swirled and flowed in a dance unlike any she'd seen. She smiled beneath the water as she drifted – they were intoxicating in their beauty and it all made sense.

Samantha's head broke the surface when Jolie lifted her.

"You're real," Samantha gasped, choking as water and tears clogged her throat.

"Of course we're real. We told you we believed in mermaids," Mirra said, pressing her hand to Samantha's chest. Instantly her coughing subsided, and she floated there, held gently between the two as the moonlight serenaded their beauty.

"Have I gone mad?" Samantha whispered.

"We all go a little mad sometimes…" Mirra quoted.

"You're crazy if you leave that man and fly home to a life you hate." Jolie cut right to the chase.

"But… I barely know him. How can I trust him?" Samantha sputtered, still trying to wrap her head around the fact that she was floating in the ocean with two mermaids.

"I thought you'd channeled your inner mermaid. That you were finally listening to your heart. What do you want, Samantha?" Mirra whispered.

"Oh god… I want… I want to believe in mermaids." Samantha laughed as tears streamed down her face. "I want to believe in love at first sight, and new beginnings, and that you can start over no matter what happens in life. That every day is a chance to be a new you. I want to stay here and swim in the ocean with you and know that two of my best friends are magick."

"And so you shall," Jolie said, kissing her full on the mouth in her joy. "Now, take my breath, and we'll show you magick."

"Take your breath?" Samantha asked, and as she opened her mouth, Jolie blew into it and then tugged her below the surface.

It was a kaleidoscope ride on an underwater roller-coaster. That was all Samantha could think as Jolie and Mirra spirited her through the waves, the reflections coloring neon tracks in the water as they dove her deep and shot straight to the surface, dipping and rolling, until Samantha's head spun and her heart all but burst with joy.

Because if there really was a world where mermaids existed, why would she ever want to leave it?

"It's time for us to take you back," Mirra said, as they broke the surface once more.

"I… this is magick. The best kind of magick. Oh, to know a world like this exists! What power… what beauty. Thank you for showing me," Samantha gasped, overcome with the gift they'd given her. The moon bathed them in her benevolent light and Sam couldn't believe she was really floating in the dark water with two such beautiful beings.

"Your man is distraught. You must go to him," Mirra said. They swam her as near to the shore as they could, then dipped beneath the waves and out of sight. Samantha could just make out Lucas walking the shoreline, calling her name, as a distressed Pipin raced in circles.

He'd never left her, she realized. Even when he'd walked away, he'd never really left her.

So why was she leaving him?

"I'm here," Samantha called, stumbling from the water.

When Lucas saw her, he ran.

"Oh god, you're okay. Please… please don't tell me you tried to…" Lucas said, his face racked with grief as he pulled her to him, showering kisses over her face.

"No… oh no, Lucas, no. I just – god this is going to sound crazy, but I thought I saw something. A mermaid, actually," Samantha babbled. "And for some crazy reason I dove into the water. I'm sorry. I shouldn't have scared you like that."

"You can't do that to me," Lucas said, his lips finding hers. "I love you. You can't leave me like that."

And there it was, Samantha thought, pressing her

face to his chest. Just like that. All she had to do was believe.

And if this was a world where mermaids existed and a man like Lucas loved her, then Samantha knew she'd found her home.

The rest of it, she'd figure out… one slow island day at a time.

EPILOGUE

"Yes!" Lola shrieked in her ear the next morning when Samantha called her from the hammock swing on Lucas's patio. Lucas smiled at her from across the patio, where he was drinking a cup of coffee and working on his laptop.

"I love you," Samantha mouthed to him, and he blew her a kiss. It still made her giddy to say it, but seeing as how they'd repeated it to each other throughout the night – they'd barely slept – she was getting more comfortable with it.

"So, what do you need me to do? Pack all your stuff? I'll bring it down myself. I have to come meet this man," Lola laughed, absolutely delighted.

"I quit my job," Samantha said, barely able to contain the big news. Lola shrieked again while Lucas applauded from across the patio.

She'd told him her plan over a breakfast croissant

earlier that morning. While he'd been away on meetings yesterday, she'd half-driven, half-stalled her way to the eco-tourist villas and had met with Lisa. They'd spent an hour together, and by the end of it had come to a tentative agreement. At the time, Samantha had agreed to review their books from afar on a monthly basis – just so they had another set of eyes on them and she'd be able to spot it if anything fishy came up. If – and yesterday morning it had been a big 'if,' even when Lisa had begged her to stay – *if* she decided to move to the island, she had an opportunity for a position at the resort.

Thinking about it now made her smile. It would be entirely different to work for a couple who poured their heart and soul into their properties, and Samantha thought that was exactly what she needed. It would be nice to come in at ground level in a business where people actually cared about their product and the impact they were having on the environment around them. And maybe, just maybe, she would finally feel like a valued team member instead of just another number on a spreadsheet.

"You don't have to rush into anything," Lucas had said, pulling her close for a hug.

"I know, but it isn't the actual job that I don't like. I love working with numbers and organizing all the systems. I'm just burnt out on being overlooked and overworked."

"This sounds perfect then," Lucas said. "But only if

you want to do it. Try it out on a temporary basis. Take your time with it. I'm worried you'll burn out again and hightail it off to another island for some other handsome lonely bachelor on the beach."

Delighted with him, and the world in general, she'd pulled him to the bedroom to show him just how unlikely that scenario was.

Smiling at the memory, she stretched her arms lazily above her head.

"You've got a job already! This is amazing," Lola gushed. "Have you told your parents?"

"I… well. I told them that I've met someone and that I'll be staying down here for a while. I also said I've accepted a new position in luxury eco-tourism. Between all the bombshells I dropped, I don't think they really knew what to say. My mother asked if I was renouncing my citizenship." Samantha sighed and pinched her nose.

"Sounds about right. I guess it's too much to hope they'll be happy for you," Lola said.

"That's okay, I'm going to learn to change my expectations of them. I think the best thing is that I'm happy for me," Samantha said and beamed over at Lucas, who was lecturing Pipin for stealing a scrap of bacon from his plate when he wasn't looking.

"That's all I've ever wanted for you," Lola said, and sighed in delight. "This is the best kind of story. Way more interesting than your spreadsheet stories."

"Hey!"

"I'm just saying… I love a good love story," Lola laughed.

"I guess I do too," Samantha laughed, fingering the mermaid pendant at her neck.

She would never share that moment with anyone, but forever after, whenever she put her mermaid comb in her hair, she promised herself she would go forth and wreak as much magick on the world as she could.

Because in the end, that was all that mattered, really – believing that, just under the surface, lay a world of magick.

AFTERWORD

I'm delighted to be writing a new series, set against the backdrop of the Caribbean island that I am blessed to live on. Hopefully this series will bring you joy and, maybe, if one day you find yourself by the sea, you'll look out to the horizon with the hopes of seeing a mermaid.

Would you like to visit the islands?

I have lovingly put together a free "Mermaid View" book with my own underwater photography. I took these photographs while diving, and the book is full of color and joy so you may want to download it to your computer or color tablet. I will also send you occasional emails with more Island Life photos along with updates on my newest books. I hope you enjoy the photos as much as I enjoyed taking them. Sparkle on, Sirens!

Download your free copy of 'Mermaid View'

https://offer.triciaomalley.com/88v21p6s0i

I hope my books have added a little magick into your life. If you have a moment to add some to my day, you can help by telling your friends and leaving a review. Word-of-mouth is the most powerful way to share my stories. Thank you.

Up to No Good: The Siren Island Series Book 2 - Available now as an e-book, paperback, or audiobook!

The following is an excerpt from Up to No Good

Book 2 in The Siren Island Series

CHAPTER 1

Lola didn't open her eyes as she felt the sheets move, her lover rolling from the bed. She steadied her breathing, listening as he used the bathroom and dressed quickly in the early morning light. The apartment door squeaked, hinges worn with age, the tell-tale sign that once more a man was leaving her life.

"And thank god for that," Lola said out loud, stretching decadently in the sheets that tangled around her still-naked body. Lola adhered to a strict "love 'em and leave 'em" policy that suited her lifestyle down to the bone. The few times she'd danced too closely to the flames of love, Lola had pirouetted away, with only a few singe marks on her heart.

It was better that way.

With so many men to sample, and so many places to visit, Lola approached life like the smorgasbord it was –

with gusto and great enthusiasm. So what if she rarely stayed in one country or kept a relationship for longer than a few months? If anything, it provided her with diverse life experiences and enough knowledge of men to know how to get while the getting was good.

She'd been restless of late.

Not that being restless was anything new to her – it typically signaled that it was time for her to move on.

Lola leaned across the bed and unlatched the arched window, its wood dented and splintered with age and use, and swung it open. Propping herself on the pillows, she casually rolled a cigarette – a habit she only indulged in when visiting France or Italy. Lighting it, she watched as a thin curl of smoke danced in a slim ray of sunlight. Below, a child called out in rapid Italian, his mother responding harshly, and slowly the small fishing village hugging the coast of the Mediterranean sprang to life.

There were worse ways to wake up, Lola mused. And yet, the scene had lost its charm for her. For a brief moment, Lola allowed herself to wallow in melancholy as she listened to friends and family greet each other on the narrow cobblestone street beneath the apartment.

The life she'd cultivated was a rich and fascinating one, Lola thought, as smoke curled into the air around her.

So why did she feel so empty?

Continue Reading

ALSO BY TRICIA O'MALLEY

STAND ALONE NOVELS

Ms. Bitch

"Ms. Bitch is sunshine in a book! An uplifting story of fighting your way through heartbreak and making your own version of happily-ever-after."

~Ann Charles, USA Today Bestselling Author

One Way Ticket

A funny and captivating beach read where booking a one-way ticket to paradise means starting over, letting go, and taking a chance on love…one more time

10 out of 10 - The BookLife Prize

Firebird Award Winner

Pencraft Book of the year 2021

THE SIREN ISLAND SERIES

ALSO BY TRICIA O'MALLEY

Good Girl

Up to No Good

A Good Chance

Good Moon Rising

Too Good to Be True

A Good Soul

A Good Heart

Available in audio, e-book & paperback!

Available from Amazon

"Love her books and was excited for a totally new and different one! Once again, she did NOT disappoint! Magical in multiple ways and on multiple levels. Her writing style, while similar to that of Nora Roberts, kicks it up a notch!! I want to visit that island, stay in the B&B and meet the gals who run it! The characters are THAT real!!!" - Amazon Review

THE ISLE OF DESTINY SERIES

ALSO BY TRICIA O'MALLEY

Stone Song

Sword Song

Spear Song

Sphere Song

A completed series.

Available in audio, e-book & paperback!

"Love this series. I will read this multiple times. Keeps you on the edge of your seat. It has action, excitement and romance all in one series."

- Amazon Review

THE ALTHEA ROSE SERIES

ALSO BY TRICIA O'MALLEY

One Tequila

Tequila for Two

Tequila Will Kill Ya (Novella)

Three Tequilas

Tequila Shots & Valentine Knots (Novella)

Tequila Four

A Fifth of Tequila

A Sixer of Tequila

Seven Deadly Tequilas

Eight Ways to Tequila

A completed series.

Available in audio, e-book & paperback!

"Not my usual genre but couldn't resist the Florida Keys setting. I was hooked from the first page. A fun read with just the right amount of crazy! Will definitely follow this series."- Amazon Review

THE MYSTIC COVE SERIES

ALSO BY TRICIA O'MALLEY

Wild Irish Heart

Wild Irish Eyes

Wild Irish Soul

Wild Irish Rebel

Wild Irish Roots: Margaret & Sean

Wild Irish Witch

Wild Irish Grace

Wild Irish Dreamer

Wild Irish Christmas (Novella)

Wild Irish Sage

Wild Irish Renegade

Available in audio, e-book & paperback!

"I have read thousands of books and a fair percentage have been romances. Until I read Wild Irish Heart, I never had a book actually make me believe in love."- Amazon Review

CONTACT ME

Love books? What about fun giveaways? Nope? Okay, can I entice you with underwater photos and cute dogs? Let's stay friends, receive my emails and contact me by signing up at my website

www.triciaomalley.com

Or find me on Facebook and Instagram.
@triciaomalleyauthor

Author's Acknowledgement

A very deep and heartfelt *thank you* goes to those in my life who have continued to support me on this wonderful journey of being an author. At times, this job can be very stressful, however, I'm grateful to have the sounding board of my friends who help me through the trickier moments of self-doubt. An extra-special thanks goes to The Scotsman, who is my number one supporter and always manages to make me smile.

Please know that every book I write is a part of me, and I hope you feel the love that I put into my stories. Without my readers, my work means nothing, and I am grateful that you all are willing to share your valuable time with the worlds I create. I hope each book brings a smile to your face and for just a moment it gives you a much-needed escape.

Slainté, Tricia O'Malley

Made in the USA
Middletown, DE
20 July 2023